Erin lowered her voice and leaned toward him.

Her lips were closer to his face than he was comfortable with. If she just leaned in a little closer…

"He asked me to marry him."

"What?" Garwin pulled his gaze from her lips to her eyes. "He did?"

"Oh yes," Erin said, "I would be Erin Chan right now if I hadn't taken a run for it."

"But why did you run?" Garwin asked, puzzled. "And how on earth did you get access to Rafi Chan?"

"It's a long story," Erin sighed, "but let me tell you, I am completely and utterly reviled by men who look like you."

Garwin swallowed. "Say that again?"

"I am sorry," Erin stood up, "it's not really you. You are a nice guy, Garwin; you are a good chef and boss. It's just that I have difficulty getting over your face."

NO TIME TO LOVE

BRENDA BARRETT

NO TIME TO LOVE
A Jamaica Treasures Book/January 2024
Published by Jamaica Treasures
Manchester, Jamaica

This is a work of fiction. Names, characters, places, and incidents are either the product of the author's imagination or are used fictitiously. Any resemblance to an actual person or persons, living or dead, events, or locales is entirely coincidental.

ISBN 978-976-97248-1-5

ABOUT THE AUTHOR

Brenda Barrett is an award-winning and bestselling author who has a passion for writing real Jamaican romances.

When she's not weaving words that transport readers to exotic locales, you can find her nurturing her green thumb in the garden or doting on her beloved cats.

With an infectious zest for life, this author brings a unique perspective to her writing that is both relatable and thought-provoking.

Don't be surprised if you find yourself lost in the pages of her latest work, as she seamlessly blends romance with some drama, mystery, and suspense, or even sci-fi, leaving readers wanting more.

You can connect with Brenda online at:
Brenalbar.com
Twitter.com/AuthorWriterBB
Facebook.com/AuthorBrendaBarrett

His tastes was more modern, and he didn't want a place with so much land to look after.

"Hey," Patti knocked on his glass.

He wound down the window and smiled at her. "Hey. Congrats on that piece you did in the paper today; it made for a good read."

"Thank you," Patti smiled.

"Tell me about Rafi Chan," Garwin stepped out of the bus and locked it. "Does he look that much like me?"

Patti nodded. "You have a family resemblance."

"So he is not exactly awful looking, then?" Garwin asked.

"I would say," Patti said. "You are not exactly awful looking."

Garwin grinned. "I wasn't fishing for a compliment. Erin said she has a hard time getting over my face. Because of Rafi Chan."

"Is that so?" Patti widened her eyes. "I didn't know she knew him."

"Yep. He asked her to marry him. She despises him." Garwin sighed. "I have no idea why this distresses me so."

"Maybe because you like her," Patti suggested. "And she doesn't like you back. This might be a first for you. Females of all ages are always throwing themselves at you. You have good-looking genes on both sides of your family tree."

"It can be a blessing and a curse," Garwin shrugged. "Why do you assume that I like Erin, though? I may be a little taken aback that I work closely with her and she finds me repulsive all because of that Rafi fellow. You need to find out how I can fix this, short of plastic surgery."

Patti grinned. "Is that so?"

"She talks to you," Garwin said, "she was your friend in high school."

"Okay," Patti sighed. "I will talk to her, but the Erin I knew in high school is a different person now. She is a bit more guarded and secretive. I didn't even know she knew Rafi Chan. Obviously, out of the two of us, you are the person she felt more comfortable telling that to.

"Maybe she only told me to cut me down a peg or two, to make me think about it all night." Garwin gritted his teeth. "She is smart. Now I can't stop thinking about her and why she doesn't like me. It is driving me crazy."

"I'd say," Patti nodded. "Or she definitely had a thing with Rafi and genuinely dislikes him, and it spilled over onto you."

"I don't like Rafi Chan," Garwin growled.

"You sound jealous," Patti laughed. "So, how does it feel?"

"How does what feel?" Garwin frowned.

"Loving somebody, and they don't love you back. It must be a novel thing for you."

"Who said anything about love?" Garwin smirked. "I have no time for love."

"I hear you," Patti said, a healthy dose of disbelief lacing her tone.

"It's true," Garwin said. "I am too busy, and with Gersham leaving for a couple of months, I think I will be even busier."

"You can afford not to be so busy," Patti said. "You don't have to be on a constant hustle anymore. So, I do not believe that excuse. If you like Erin, you should do something about it. You deserve to be happy."

Chapter Two

He deserved to be happy. Garwin thought about that while he was putting on his football gear. He had a coaching session with the Crimson Hill Prep football club that was under his tutelage. They were heading for the regional finals. They had a friendly game with Burberry Prep, which he and the Burberry Coach had agreed would be a learning experience. He should be thinking about that; instead, he wondered if he was ready for a serious relationship.

He probably was; he was beginning to find his short-lived flings tiresome. Not that he had that many of them. He had been short on time for anything romantic these past couple of years. His whole philosophy had been to hustle hard and make money. Then, he could give himself over to the finer feelings if he was blessed to find anyone who would be right. He hadn't been against romance; he just thought he had little incentive to pursue it. He had to want to; he had to be motivated.

His friends were coupled up and married—Derrick and Cindy, Camille and Leighton, Jack and Cambria, Nicky and Orandy, Mercedes and Charles. One after the other, they had tied the knot.

He would be lying if he said he didn't feel left out of all the love connections around him. Every other month for the past two years, he catered a wedding for one of his friends. It had even started to infect his family since Gersham was now married to Patti Sue. Patti had been the only woman Gersham had ever loved, and his fixation on her puzzled Garwin.

When they had broken up, Garwin had repeatedly asked Gersham, "Why don't you just move on? Replace her."

"Nobody is irreplaceable." Gersham had stoically maintained. That kind of attitude had always baffled him until Erin walked into his life six months ago with her no-nonsense attitude, casual friendliness, and zero interest in him. He was feeling stirrings of feelings he couldn't name.

He feared he had an obsession. Where did this feeling come from?

He remembered her from high school. She had been two grades below him. He had thought of her as Mercedes' little mousy friend who barely answered when he said hello and always seemed to be shrinking behind her friends when he showed up.

Mercedes had even told him once that Erin liked him a lot, and he had dismissed it. The girls who liked him didn't keep him at a distance. All the girls had found him fascinating in high school. On a whim, he had grown his hair long, which had been an endless fascination for them.

Admittedly, he had liked the attention that had brought him, but he hadn't taken advantage of the attention, he didn't have a girlfriend in high school. He had been everybody's friend, popular, well-liked.

He talked to girls, they talked to him, but there had never been anyone special. On Valentine's Day, he was usually inundated with gifts, but he never got anyone anything; he had not wanted to give them the wrong impression.

He had played football for his school and was one of their star strikers. Football had occupied much of his time in the latter part of high school. Life was usually school, then after-school football practice, and the restaurant. He and Gersham had been responsible for cleaning all the pots and pans after the restaurant closed in the evenings. It was hard work.

His schedule had no place for romance; even if he had liked someone, he wouldn't have had the space or time for them. He couldn't invite them home either. Home for him had not been a refuge.

When his father came from prison, it had been especially awkward. Sterling would just sit and stare at nothing for hours, sometimes bursting into tears at the most random times. It had been depressing. His friends had found it unsettling. He went to their house instead or hung out at Crimson Hill Great House; Maud would allow them to use the gazebo as their hangout spot as long as they didn't get too rowdy.

He got into the restaurant van and made a mental note that he needed to pick up his newly bought vehicle from Montego Bay sometime this week. Having a personal vehicle was long overdue.

He turned on the radio and listened to music as he headed to Crimson Hill Prep. It wasn't a long drive, just seven minutes from where he lived. It was close to the restaurant, too; he would have left the restaurant to go to the school if he had remembered to carry his coaching gear.

He had gotten roped into coaching the boys at the prep school by his old coach from high school, Aaron Cole. He had said yes because he couldn't deny Aaron anything; he had been a stabilizing force in Garwin's life while growing up.

He groaned when he drove up to the school and saw Maura Hunt. She was a teacher there. She was a pint-sized beauty who was used to wearing sky-high heels so that she could look taller than her students. She was not interested in football, so she was there to see him.

They had an on-and-off situation for the past year. She had ended things with an ultimatum: marry me, or else we don't see each other anymore. He had taken the second option of not seeing her anymore.

He didn't want to marry her. He couldn't picture a long-term relationship with Maura. She had been a convenient outlet for his sexual needs. He hadn't made her any promises. In fact, they had agreed to just go with the flow. She was a divorcee who had claimed she never wanted to marry again. He had liked it like that. Her ultimatum had come out of left field. He didn't miss her; he hadn't even thought much about her since that time, especially since he was preoccupied with Erin.

She waved to him when he came out of the vehicle.

He waved back, grabbed his gear, and locked the van when she came behind him.

"I changed my mind, Garwin."

"Huh," he looked at her, dazed.

"I shouldn't have given you that ultimatum. I am sorry."

"It's been six months," Garwin shrugged, "I have since moved on. I hoped you had, too."

"Wait," Maura frowned, "who are you seeing now?"

"It's none of your business," Garwin smiled at her to take the sting out of his words.

She walked behind him, "I am not seeing anyone."

"Sorry to hear," Garwin said, "I hope that changes shortly."

"I want what we had," Maura said, "I miss you; I miss us."

Garwin stopped. "You told me you had too much self-respect to be with a man who only wanted you for sex. You said you wanted more. I didn't want more, so I made my exit."

Maura glared at him, "I didn't expect you to leave! I've been waiting for you to come back to me. It's hard to find the right person in these hills; all the eligible single men are taken."

"It's too late now," Garwin said, "I am interested in someone else; I can't stop thinking about her. I think I may be a little bit obsessed."

Maura opened her mouth in awe. "Say what? You don't obsess."

"I didn't," Garwin sighed, "apparently there is a first time for everything."

Maura stared at him speechlessly. "I can't believe this. She must be dynamite in bed."

"I haven't even kissed her," Garwin said, "and she hates my face."

"Now I know you are pulling my leg; no woman would say that," Maura grimaced, "you could have just told me to get lost instead of concocting this story."

She spun around and left him.

****

Erin's bicycle was there when he drove up to the restaurant. It was late, a couple of minutes after eight. His team had won the evenly played match, and all the players were treated to ice cream by the school. He was quite proud of them; coaching was not as boring as he had thought it would be but rather thrilling.

It was nice to be a role model for boys that age, like how Coach Cole had been for him. And now he was ravenous. He hoped for leftovers, but the dinner crowd was still sizeable, with a few minutes left until closing. Maybe there wouldn't be any leftovers. It was known to happen on some days.

He anticipated seeing Erin again; she was responsible for closing the store tonight, so she would still be there. She sat alone in the courtyard, staring at her device and giggling. The kitchen was winding down, and she was already wearing street clothes.

"Hey," he sat across from her.

"Hey, Chef," she grinned, "look at this video."

It was a video of a drunken cat. Garwin frowned. "I've seen it. I don't find it funny."

"Oh, sorry," Erin frowned, "oh no, I forgot about your aversion to drunks."

"Not just drunks; it's cruelty to animals. Whatever they did to cause that cat to stumble around like that is not a laughing matter. That animal is in distress."

"Oh yes, I never thought of that. It really is not funny when you see it that way," Erin said, a mortified expression on her face.

"Don't sweat it; I am extra sensitive to anything that looks remotely abusive to animals or humans, especially children."

"Yes," Erin nodded, "I can see how you can be extra alert to that kind of thing."

"I am going to see if I can get some leftovers," he said.

"Wait, were you playing football?" Erin asked, "You look

remarkably unruffled for someone who was playing.”

“Not playing, coaching,” Garwin said. “I coach the Crimson Hill Tigers. And I must say, we are not too shabby.”

Erin grinned. “I didn’t know this about you.”

“There are a lot of things you don’t know about me,” Garwin said, “do you want to know more?”

Erin frowned. “Are you flirting with me, Chef?”

“I am,” Garwin nodded, “and my name is Garwin. I want you to start calling my name. I no longer answer to chef from you. As for Rafi Chan, we may resemble each other, but we are nothing alike. So you better start liking my face.”

“Okay,” Erin said weakly.

Garwin smiled. “I expected a rousing disagreement, not a meek okay.”

“I know you are nothing like Rafi Chan, and I have been calling you chef to put some distance between us,” Erin shrugged, “you called my bluff.”

“Good,” Garwin nodded. “Now I am going to scrape the bottom of the pots for something to eat. Wait for me; you can keep me company.”

****

“So what was it like being engaged to Rafi Chan?” Garwin sat down across from Erin; his plate was piled high with leftovers.

“I thought we were going to talk about you,” Erin said, cupping her hand under her chin, “you said you would tell me more about you.”

“My adult life is pretty standard and uneventful,” Garwin shrugged, “yours, on the other hand, sounds exciting.”

Erin chuckled. “But there are things I have always wondered about you that I need to know. For instance, why didn't you ever date Mercedes?"

"She feels like family," Garwin said, "when we were kids, we spent a lot of time together. I have never viewed her in a romantic light. I have never had a romantic relationship."

"Lies," Erin shook her head. "Garwin Silver has never had a romantic relationship. Not buying it."

"It's true," Garwin said, "I understand romance to mean a deep emotional connection that goes beyond sex. I have never had that. You know that song by Bryan Adams, 'Everything I Do, I Do It for You'?"

"Yes," Erin nodded.

"Well, that epitomizes romance for me," Garwin said, "to say to someone, 'I'll fight for you, I'll lie for you, walk the wire for you, I'd die for you,' is true love."

Erin raised an eyebrow, "So, you're saying you've never felt that for anyone?"

Garwin sighed, "Nope. Never."

"Neither have I," Erin said. "What you just described is what everybody fantasizes about for themselves. But it's just that—a fantasy. You make do with who you have around and pray they don't become monsters after they have locked you into a commitment."

"Oh wow," Garwin raised an eyebrow, "Rafi was that bad huh."

"The worst!" Erin shuddered. "He has made me see people in a different light. I mean, I don't know if I'll ever be trusting people again. How can I take anyone at face value? I'll always be waiting for the other shoe to fall. I'd probably always hold my breath, waiting for the big reveal. Uh, I can't stand that guy."

"Yikes," Garwin said. "Are you ever going to tell me what he did?"

"Yes," Erin nodded, "maybe, I don't know. I am trying

to forget the whole thing. I am patiently waiting until he finally gets married. Then maybe I can breathe a sigh of relief. I am a little paranoid where he is concerned."

"Why?" Garwin asked.

"Because I don't know, he might come after me," Erin sighed. "He'll want to know why I broke it off with him; I only left him a note. I didn't tell him a proper goodbye. And if I see him now, I don't know what to tell him."

"I am assuming he cheated," Garwin said, "that's terrible."

"If only that was it," Erin said. "I'd be quite happy with only that."

"More than cheating?" Garwin widened his eyes. "What could be more than cheating that would make a girl hate you so badly that she doesn't even trust people anymore? Mmm."

Erin grimaced. "There are other things…"

"Mysterious, give me a hint," Garwin said, "or I will be thinking about it all of tonight."

"Erin," Mabel called from the kitchen, "since you are the chef in charge for tomorrow, I need some guidance here!"

"Saved by the may bell," Garwin murmured.

Erin chuckled. "That's quite a play on words there."

"That's my specialty," Garwin smiled. "Something else you didn't know about me: I am the reigning champion in my family with the play-on-words game."

Erin laughed and got up. "Is that so?"

"Yup, even Garnet, who reads four novels per week, can't beat me. I'll carry the game tomorrow night after work," Garwin said. "Maybe then we'll pick up the conversation."

"Okay," Erin smiled.

Chapter Three

Erin stared at the latest affirmation she had placed on the dresser mirror with yellow post-it notes. She was standing in the cramped little room she called home, preparing for work. Last night had been fun with Garwin; he was different from all the other guys she had ever talked to. After working with him for six months, she had gotten glimpses of the kind of man he was, but it was good to talk to him without her barriers.

He was honest to a fault, sensitive, kind, and considerate. And she had happily called him Garwin. She couldn't deny that when she returned to Crimson Hill, Garwin was the first person she thought about seeing. She had wondered if something could happen between them. She had fantasized that maybe this time was their chance.

She had been fixated on him when she was younger; it was a wonder that she hadn't allowed her nonchalant attitude toward him to crack in the last six months. It was amazing that he didn't see behind her act. She had forced herself to equate him with Rafi Chan, but that hadn't worked.

She didn't want to think about Rafi Chan just now; instead, she focused on her affirmation. "I am worthy of being loved, being happy, and doing what brings me joy," she said out loud.

"Modern graffiti," her grandmother said behind her. "Why do you post those things all over the mirror? What do you need all of those sayings for?"

"Morning Gan Gan," Erin sighed, "what can I do for you today?"

Moving back home to her grandmother was exactly how she had imagined and dreaded, and it was all Rafi Chan's fault. She was only here because he did not know she had a Crimson Hills link or was close to her grandmother. He knew about her parents and that they lived in the Cayman Islands. He probably thought she would run to them. This was probably the last place that he'd look for her.

Staying with Bettina Lounds, or Miss Betty to the community and Gan Gan to her grandchildren, had been necessary. As expected, it had taken her a good part of six months to get used to her grandmother's personality again. It wasn't that her grandmother was a particularly bad person. She was kind to a fault and very family-oriented; it's just that she was severely outdated in her thinking, truly old-fashioned, distrustful of progress or anything outside her comfort zone, and loudly opinionated even when she was wrong.

Miss Betty folded her arms and said wryly, "Morning, you didn't answer me; why do you have those little notes posted all over the mirror?"

Erin sighed and looked at her grandmother. "These are my morning affirmations; they are a good thing, not graffiti."

"Hmph," Miss Betty snorted. "New age nonsense. We didn't do any of that back in my day and still knew we were worthy and whatever."

Erin opened her mouth to protest and then closed it back. It didn't make sense to argue with her grandmother.

"Anyway," Miss Betty said, "I came to tell you that your cousin Serena and her three children are coming over this week, which means you must share the room."

"With all four of them?" Erin widened her eyes. "No way."

"No, silly," Miss Betty said, "maybe Serena will share with you; the children can have the other room with the bunk bed and the single."

"Why is she staying here?" Erin asked. "Aunty Sandy lives around the corner. Her mother is literally next door."

"Sandy doesn't have the space, I do," Miss Betty said. "If she doesn't stay here, she will be on the streets; her landlord is kicking her out tomorrow."

"He can't just kick her out!" Erin said. "That's unconscionable."

"He gave her notice three months ago," Miss Betty shrugged. "Serena ignored him, so he is taking drastic measures."

"Scatterbrained Serena," Erin muttered, "where is her boyfriend in all of this?"

"They broke up. He got married and lives in Montego Bay with his new wife," Miss Betty said. "She can't stay with him under the circumstances now, can she?"

"No, I guess not," Erin said, "how long will she be staying?"

"Until she finds another place," Miss Betty said. "She knows she can't stay here forever. I offer shelter to my kin who need it, including you. But this three-bedroom house is never empty. After having four children and seeing them past the worst, with all of them having their own place, I would have some peace and quiet, but it's not happening; their children keep cluttering up my space."

"I didn't know you all would make this a one-way stop. A refugee camp," Miss Betty mumbled. "And I don't mind," she added, "once you guys pay your bills. I'm a retiree on a fixed income."

Erin resisted the urge to roll her eyes. She had heard this before. She had heard it when she had just entered high school, and her parents had left her with Miss Betty while they migrated to Cayman to work.

It had been her mother's idea not to pull her out of school to go live with them because they had left in the middle of her first semester of high school. She ended up staying four years until she finished high school.

Her older brother, Nigel, had his final year of high school but opted to stay with an uncle in Falmouth. He had stubbornly refused to stay here. He had preferred to travel every day to school in Crimson Hills.

"Grandmothers are nicer when you don't live with them," Nigel had said.

And boy, was he right. Miss Betty was on another level of eccentricity. Several times in the three years when she lived with her grandmother, she had ceased the chance to stay at other people's houses just to escape her. She had stayed over at Mercedes and Patti Sue's house as often as they invited her, and she would go off to Cayman as soon as the holidays came around.

She had vowed that she wouldn't come back and stay with her. But here she was. Another thing to blame Rafi Chan for. She had thought she would never live with Gan Gan again. But it was six months running, and the speeches about her house being a refugee camp were becoming more frequent.

Erin gave her a good chunk of money monthly; she called it rent. It had two uses: it kept Miss Betty from snooping in her business and not asking many questions an it reduced the number of mentions that she was a retiree on a fixed income, but apparently, the novelty of getting extra cash was wearing off.

What on earth was Miss Betty doing with the money? Erin wondered. She got regular cash injections from all her children except Sandy, who had eight children and was stretched thin.

Her uncle Morris was a lawyer in Kingston, her father Marshall was a banker in Cayman, and her aunt Phyllis was a dentist in Montego Bay. They all took care of their mother. They were a close-knit family, too.

Erin sighed; she could have opted to stay with Morris in Kingston or Phyllis in Montego Bay. Her uncle and aunt would be happy to have her stay with them, but that would be begging for Rafi to find her. He would find her in a heartbeat if she worked in Kingston or Montego Bay. Crimson Hills was a more obscure place.

"Ehem," Miss Betty said, "you have that spaced-out look on your face again."

"I was just thinking," Erin focused on her grandmother. "I will make way for Serena today when I return from work. I could also find a place where I don't have to share. I do pay you market value rent."

"No!" Miss Betty said, alarmed. "It wouldn't be right for you to live some other place when you have me here. There is room."

She didn't want to lose her monthly chunk of money.

Erin sighed. "I thought I had outgrown all of this. How will the sleeping arrangements go?" She looked at the two single beds in the room. "I'd be sharing with Serena as if we are twelve again. I don't have to stay here."

"It will just be for a little while," Miss Betty said placatingly. "Serena will find a place, and you will be alone again."

"I am dreading this," Erin said. "Serena's children are noisy. I visited her the other day, and I couldn't get a word in; her little girls are extra chatty, and the boy is always making loud gun noises and screeching, 'I'll kill you.'

"Why does he feel a need to be shooting things and shouting that, and why does his mother let him? I don't know. Where did he learn that from?"

"The television," Miss Betty said heavily. "Serena allows them to watch anything. I talk to her about it, but she doesn't listen. When they are watching television, she gets her quiet time. Who can blame her? I was a single mother with four children, and they were a handful. I wouldn't want to be growing children in this day and age; it is not easy."

Erin sighed. If she didn't get a move on, this would turn into her grandmother talking about children nowadays, and she didn't have time for that.

"Okay, I'm going to work. I'm taking your bicycle again."

"No problem," Miss Betty said. "I must stop by and tell Garwin Silver that the food has been especially good lately."

Erin grinned. "That would be lying; you don't eat out. Everyone knows that you wouldn't be caught dead at a restaurant."

"But I've heard," Miss Betty said. "People have been saying there's an extra oomph to the food."

Erin smiled. "You still listening to those people in your head?"

Miss Betty guffawed.

Erin went to the side of the house where the bicycle was. One of the tires was obviously deflated. She had known something was wrong when she came in last night. She should have woken up earlier and checked the wheel, but she couldn't address the bicycle wheel now.

She would have to walk to work. She would make it on time, but barely.

She liked to be there when Garwin was opening the store. They usually had coffee together and chit-chatted about their tasks for the day.

Her hours were fairly reasonable in her opinion; she worked from six to two thirty most days. She and Garwin took turns with the breakfast and lunch service. Gersham usually did dinner.

When they had additional events to cater for, which seemed like an everyday occurrence, she would stay behind for those. But basically, she saw Garwin every day for hours at a time. One would think the novelty of it would wear off, but it was still there at the surface.

Who knew that Garwin would be her work colleague?

In high school, she had elaborate fantasies about her and Garwin. She couldn't even speak to any of her friends about some of them. They were too intense.

Back then, he didn't even look her way. There were too many females fawning over him for him to notice her anyway. That was probably why when Rafi Chan, a man who resembled Garwin quite a bit, paid her some attention, she was bowled over.

And now that she was repelled by Rafi she was trying to convince herself she was also repelled by Garwin. Which was a joke; Garwin just needed to crack a smile, one of his slow half-smiles, and she felt hot, like she was chopping up pepper in a hundred-degree kitchen.

She was an adult woman, twenty-six years old. She had kissed a couple of frogs, thought what she thought would be the prince, and ended up broken-hearted and fleeing for her life. She couldn't forget that part.

The reason why she was back home, working at Silver Spoon restaurant, and pretending to dislike Garwin Silver was because of Rafi Chan. She started down the road and allowed her mind to wander.

Chapter Four

Sometime in the past

"I hate to do this, Erin," Mark looked at her after calling her into his office.

"Do what?" Erin asked.

"This weekend, I am going to have to give the restaurant to you to run."

Erin clapped her hands in glee. "Yay! It's not the first time."

"Yeah, but it's the first time I'm having such a high-profile client book out for the whole weekend, and I'm not here to oversee things."

Mark drummed his fingers on the desk. "This is the stuff of nightmares. Cami has a C-section scheduled for this weekend. I have to be there for her. I promised her that if we signed up to have this kid, I'd be there every step of the way. What am I doing having a kid at 54?" He held his head in his hands.

Erin cleared her throat. "This will be a walk in the park. I've run this place before without you around. I did it for a full month when you went on vacation with Cami."

"But it is Ralph Rogan," Mark said, "Head of the billionaire Rogans, my former boss."

"Never heard of them," Erin shrugged.

"Which kitchen cellar have you been living under?" Mark asked.

"This one?" Erin laughed. "I've been working here since culinary school."

"And you are a good chef."

"The best, you have always said." Erin reminded Mark smugly.

"Yeah, you were born for it," Mark nodded. "However, I don't want Ralph Rogan to realize that I'm not here and leaving just a 24-year-old kid in my place."

"What's with you and this ageism?" Erin asked. "You can't have a kid at 54. I can't run a restaurant at 24."

"Okay," Mark held up his hand. "You have a point. You have run this place on weekends and that month and nothing happened. This is not even a large party. It's a small one. Ralph is having his son and some of his closest friends come here for a birthday party. It shouldn't be a big deal. His son's name is Rich."

"Cute," Erin smirked. "Rich Rogan. Why doesn't anyone call their kid Poor?"

Mark laughed. "Anyway, we'll run through the procedure, which is the norm, to satisfy my peace of mind. You'll have to give a speech with the cake. You wheel it out, make sure your uniform is in tip-top shape, and you give a one-liner or two saying, 'Rich, I hope this birthday is one to remember,' you cut it with a huge knife, and they cheer."

"Don't worry, Mark, it seems simple enough," Erin said.

"Everything will be quite fine."

It wasn't. She had thought Rich Rogan was a kid, probably twelve years old. How was she to know he was celebrating his twenty-seventh birthday with his friends, most of whom were male? All of them were rich and, according to Nina, who was serving as sous chef, handsome bar none. Erin got to see for herself when she wheeled out the giant cake.

As Nina had said, there really was an inordinate number of handsome men. One of them caught her eye. He looked a lot like Garwin Silver from Crimson Hills. She hadn't thought about Garwin for years. Her unrequited crush. The familiar longing came rushing back to her when she thought about him.

She made eye contact with the guy more than once, and then she left the eating area with her heart maddeningly pounding. He wasn't exactly a Garwin Silver clone, but he had to be a relative. They had the same-shaped face, level brows, and Romanesque nose. There were subtle differences, though, that set them apart. The stranger's hair was straight, whereas Garwin's was wavy, and Garwin was a tad darker than he was. Maybe the mouth was similar, too, with a fullish lower lip and an inviting smile? She hadn't really stopped to stare at his mouth for too long.

Was she destined to like men looking like Garwin? Was this a curse?

She went to the kitchen with her hands shaking and her head throbbing. Nina took one look at her and laughed. "I told you they were handsome."

Erin nodded. "They are. Who is that Indian one with the caramel skin and satirical smile?"

"Rafi Chan," Nina said without a pause, "Jamaica's most eligible bachelor. His parents won't allow him to marry just anyone. I guess it has to be a girl from India, from one of their old neighborhoods.

"According to the gossip rags, Rafi is resisting marriage so far. There are rumors that he wants to marry for love, not duty like his whole family."

"That's so sweet," Erin nodded.

"There are also rumors that he doesn't care if they're black, Indian, white, or Chinese," Nina grinned. "Nor is he hung up on class. Some of his girlfriends in the past have been from all strata of society. So you and I may have a chance."

Erin smiled, "not interested. He's a less interesting-looking version of someone I used to have a crush on. Now that guy was spectacular."

"Childhood crush?" Nina asked pityingly.

"Yes," Erin nodded.

"Is he a Chan, too?"

"Nope," Erin said. "He's a Silver."

"I'd choose the Chan over the Silver because of the money and connections," Nina said. "But if your old crush is not just Silver in name and has a lot of silver…"

Erin laughed. "There is no choice to be made, and I'm tired of fantasizing. I want a nice ordinary boyfriend who loves me, and I love him, and we're compatible."

"The dream," Nina said dreamily. "I want that too. How will we find that, though, these men nowadays…" Her words petered out. Ralph Rogan entered the kitchen.

It created quite a stir.

"Erin McMillan," he bellowed.

He was a big guy with a booming voice. He looked a little like the boxer George Foreman. "I loved your speech and the food. It was delicious. Congratulations to your team, and such a wise find in you Mark has made. But I'm afraid I'm going to have to poach you. I already squared it with Mark; he protested as I knew he would, but I need you to be my personal chef in St. Lucia.

"I only hire women for my personal business," he said. He handed her his card and stepped out of the kitchen. "I'll have my secretary call you to make arrangements."

"What in the world?" Erin looked at Nina in consternation. "Is he serious?"

"He is!" Nina squealed. "I would find out what he's paying, and then I would jump on the offer like a hot potato."

Nina couldn't contain her excitement, and her eyes sparkled as she continued, "I mean, St. Lucia, Erin! It's a dream destination, and a chance to be a personal chef for someone like him could be an incredible opportunity."

Erin was still processing the unexpected turn of events. "But what about the whole 'only hiring women' thing? That seems a bit... unusual, doesn't it?"

Nina shrugged. "Well, you know how some people have their quirks and preferences. If it means fulfilling your culinary dreams in such a beautiful place, maybe it's worth making a few adjustments."

Erin nodded; Nina's excitement was contagious. "I'll look into the offer and see what he's offering regarding compensation and living arrangements. If it makes sense, I might pack my bags for St. Lucia soon."

****

Two weeks later, she ended up at Ralph Rogan's mansion in St. Lucia with Mark's blessing. She didn't know what transpired between the two men. But she was sure money changed hands. Mark was quite happy to shoo her out.

But working at the beautiful Rogan estate was an opportunity she didn't want to miss either. First, Ralph paid her three times what she was getting at All Stars restaurant.

And then there was the fact that the man only hired women for his personal staff.

She admired him for it until she learned from the staff that he only did so because he didn't want any men around his third wife, Judy. Judy was his May-December romance. She was far younger than he was, a supermodel turned stay-at-home mom.

And then it made sense. He wasn't a feminist. He was a jealous husband.

Ralph spent about a third of the year in St. Lucia with Judy, who was St. Lucian; she had two young girls, three and five. Erin was their main personal chef. Jody rarely entertained, except when Ralph was around or her stepchildren stopped by. Ralph had two children with his first wife and three with his second; all of them were adults, and some of them were older than Jody. Ralph's children lived all over the world where the businesses were. And when they came home with their children, it was like a restaurant, a busy, high-traffic restaurant.

The kitchen at the main house was a chef's dream. Erin even had staff just like at the restaurant: a sous chef and a dishwasher. Some days, it was busy and fun, especially when they entertained, and some days, Jody just required a protein shake, and the girls wanted sandwiches.

It was her first stint as a personal chef. She had heard her colleagues talk about being personal chefs before. Some of them liked it. Some didn't. She loved it. What was there not to love?

Jody was incredibly sweet. She seemed untouched by the vast wealth at her disposal. She treated the staff, including Erin, as friends hanging out with her instead of employees.

She was trying to be a writer, and she would come to the kitchen when she was bored and tell them about her storylines.

"Give me your honest opinion about the twist," she would urge.

Erin never held back her opinions, and Jody began to depend on her more. They had a friendship of sorts.

The Rogan compound was also a dream place to live, even for staff. There was the main house, which occupied but a tiny part of the eight-acre land. It was a sprawling edifice with twelve bedrooms and fifteen bathrooms. Then there were the guest accommodations, five villas with their own entrance and pool area, and the staff accommodation, which looked like a housing development. Several little cottages with white picket fences lined a picturesque street, surrounded by colorful bougainvillea.

It was idyllic. It reminded Erin of a jigsaw puzzle picture she had put together with her brother one Christmas.

Erin occupied a one-bedroom that was left vacant by the previous chef. The interior was just as charming as the exterior. It was painted white; the open plan area had a tiny living room and kitchenette and a bedroom with a double bed and some closet space.

The staff had their own swimming pool and outdoor barbecue area. The staff size increased whenever any of Raph Rogan's children arrived. They usually carried a small retinue of staff with them.

Everybody was friendly, especially Heather, Jody's personal secretary. She came to join Erin by the pool, her first week there, pulling up a lounge chair beside her and smiled.

"Hey Erin, my name is Heather; I am sometimes secretary and sometimes spy," she said to Erin candidly. "Jody needs a loyal person by her side. I must be that for her because this may look like paradise, but it is a combat zone."

"It is?" Erin widened her eyes.

"Yup," Heather grinned and raised her dark glasses to her forehead. "The other wives don't like Jody. She is young, pretty, and fertile."

"The other wives?" Erin opened her eyes.

"I mean the ex-wives," Heather grinned. "They sometimes vacation here but not in the main house. You won't be working for them; they take their own staff. They come and go to the villas as they please. Sometimes, they wander to the main house to torture Jody."

"As for the kids, all of them are horrid. Well, maybe, except for Rich. He is the best of a bad lot. I wouldn't exchange places with Jody if you paid me. No sir, never."

"Why?" Erin asked.

"She has to be alert for plots to get rid of her, bullying, backstabbing, the works. I'll tell you a secret," Heather said, "she has set up cameras all over the house so that she knows exactly what is said and done. It's a pain because I have to review it and report to her whenever they are here."

"Oh," Erin swallowed. Was that why Jody liked her? She always said complimentary things about her to the staff while in the kitchen.

It was good that she was the kind of person who always spoke well of people. She didn't say anything at all if she had nothing good to say.

"That reminds me," Heather said, "Rich is coming to stay; he will live in the main house with his friend Rafi Chan for six months. They are starting a business venture with the government; they are both excited about it."

"Okay," Erin nodded.

"I will send you their dietary requirements," Heather said, "for some strange reason, Jody is excited about having Rich around. I think he is just as bad as his siblings, but this is not my family, so I keep out of it."

Erin nodded. "As you should."

"Beware of Rafi Chan," Heather said, "I normally tell newcomers to be aware of the Rogan family friends in general. They know Ralph only hires women here because he keeps Jody in a bubble, so they all think the staff is fair game."

"The chef before this fell in love with one of them. She saw dollar signs, and happily ever after, he saw a girl to play games with. Needless to say, she got hurt severely and had to leave. Don't let it happen to you."

Heather lowered her glasses, jammed a headphone in her ear, and leaned back in the lounger.

Erin didn't get to ask her any more questions.

****

Things got busy when Rich and Rafi moved into the main house. It felt like they had a dinner party every night with various government officials and significant private investors on the island.

Rich's secretary, Lorna, contacted her daily with a menu sheet. Sometimes, the menu read like it should be in a five-star restaurant. Erin was up to the task; it was challenging and fun. She had never worked with so many expensive ingredients or gotten a chance to stretch her culinary muscles that much.

On the first night, the main course consisted of filet mignon with red wine, pan-seared Chilean Sea Bass served on a bed of saffron risotto, and, for dessert, a perfect tiramisu.

"I heard moans," Carla, the server, said. "One man who said he is a foodie and writes for some magazine said he has never had filet mignon that good. The tiramisu was a hit as well."

"Good," Erin basked in the glow of the compliment.

"They are all threatening to steal you."

"Even better," Erin laughed.

She was going out of the kitchen through the back door after another successful night of cooking when Rich Rogan and Rafi Chan strode in.

"Erin, is it?" Rich said. "I remember when Dad poached you from Mark. The best decision he has ever made."

Erin smiled. "Thank you."

Rich was tall; she hadn't seen him up close before. He was slim, caramel-skinned, with a straight-as-an-arrow nose. His face was narrow and good-looking, resembling his mother, who rumor had it was a famous model in her heyday.

"This is my friend, Rafi Chan; he wanted to meet you personally," Rich continued, giving her a thorough appraisal. Erin wished she had thought to spruce up herself on her way out. But all she had been thinking about was a bath and bed.

Rafi held out his hand and shook hers for longer than was necessary. "I fell in love with your cooking, and now, meeting you, I fall in love with you."

Erin blushed. She was sure her ears were red.

"Er… thank you."

Rafi laughed. "No, Erin, thank you for your lovely meals."

His voice was husky and smooth as honey.

She didn't know how to take it. His eyes were making her promises, boring into hers like a tunnel into unexplored depths. The ambiance around them seemed to blur, the clinking of cutlery and distant murmurs fading into the background. Rafi's hand lingered, warm against hers.

He leaned in slightly, his gaze unwavering. "Your dishes tell stories, Erin. Each flavor, every nuance, is a chapter of its own. But tonight, I want to know the story behind the chef."

Erin chuckled nervously, her fingers absentmindedly playing with the edge of her shirt. "I'm afraid my story isn't as exciting as my dishes."

Rafi's smile deepened, and he motioned toward the door. "Let me be the judge of that; I'll walk you home."

Chapter Five

Erin snapped out of her trip-down memory when a few morning joggers passed her. She exchanged pleasantries with them as was expected. Everybody was always unfailingly chirpy in the morning, especially the ones who exercised. And most of them were seeing her for the first time in conversation range. She usually rode by them and waved.

She had kept a low profile over the last six months and wasn't out of the woods yet. Rafi Chan was still at large.

She dragged her thoughts back to their grand romance.

One year before...

Rafi was a food connoisseur, and he usually found her in the kitchen, where they chatted easily. After their initial meeting, Erin became comfortable with him. He was charming and over the top, taking her around St. Lucia on their days off. They spent idyllic days snorkeling, exploring hidden coves, discovering vibrant local markets, savoring exotic fruits, and enjoying freshly caught seafood.

As the days turned into weeks, their bond deepened. Rafi admired Erin's culinary prowess, reveling in how her eyes lit up when she spoke about cooking. Erin, in turn, admired Rafi's zest for life, his adventurous spirit, and his ability to turn even the simplest moments into something extraordinary.

He usually walked her home or took the Rogan yacht out to sea on the nights after work. Erin was being spoiled, and she loved it. She enjoyed the romance of it all. Rafi was satisfied with chaste kisses and not rushing things, and she was content with that.

However, a piece of her, though caught up in the romance, was not in love with him. She felt like something was missing.

Rafi, on the other hand, liberally confessed his love every day. "This, what we have, is exactly what I was looking for," he told her, sincerity in his eyes.

Then, on her day off, he whisked her off to a private island one of his friends owned and proposed. Rafi went down on one knee, surrounded by a thousand candle lights in a gazebo. "Erin, I never expected to find someone like you. Will you marry me?" He produced a large blue diamond ring that sparkled in the half-light.

Erin had a teensy voice at the back of her head, saying, "This is going too fast. Something about this is not right." But she said yes out loud.

"Yes, I'll marry you, Rafi."

****

"I heard the great news!" Heather, Jody's secretary, was the first to approach her two days after the romantic proposal. She had knocked on the cottage door and walked in before Erin could react.

It was barely light out. Heather looked hyped.

"News travels fast," Erin said wryly, taking a step back, "I haven't told anyone yet. Not even my parents."

"Don't tell them," Heather leaned on the door and locked it. "How good are you at acting? You are going to have to treat this very smartly."

"What are you talking about?" Erin frowned.

"Jody said I should show you the video," Heather lowered her voice, "she doesn't want you getting hurt."

"What video?" Erin frowned.

"You'll soon see," Heather sighed. "What do you know about the Chan family?"

"Nothing much," Erin sat heavily across from Heather. "Rafi said they were a nice, close-knit family, and they would accept me with open arms. It would take a little warming up first..."

Heather chuckled.

"What's so funny?" Erin frowned.

"He is lying," Heather said. "They are a weird bunch and have more intrigue than a soap opera. Let me catch you up to speed on your fiancé's family. There is no way on earth that Rafi could take you home as his fiancée. They only have arranged marriages set from when they are babies. Rafi's last two arrangements fell through; one fled the country, no one knows where she is, and the other mysteriously disappeared."

"Are you serious?" Erin frowned. "Why?"

"There is a theory that Rafi scared or paid them off," Heather sighed. "Anyway, you were a convenient patsy.

He was going to take you home to the family house as a chef and convince you to poison his father. He assumes you will do it because you are in love with him and want to be together; he'll explain that his father is in the way."

"No!" Erin shook her head. "I'd never do that."

"I know," Heather said. "He is getting desperate. He was paying someone in the house to slowly poison his father, nothing too obvious. His father has cancer, and the poison was supposed to hasten his demise.

"Anyway, his father figured out that he was being poisoned and fired all the staff who would have access to his food. He is currently rehiring. Rafi thinks he can sneak you in as one of the kitchen staff. You work for Ralph; you would certainly be considered. Rafi would wholeheartedly recommend you."

"You cannot be serious!" Erin squealed.

"Keep your voice down," Heather whipped out her phone. "I have the video from the horse's mouth. I told you that Jody knows everything that goes on in that house. I am sending the video to you." Heather clicked a button on her phone.

Erin went for her phone and watched the video; her mouth couldn't quite close. Rafi was in bed with Rich; they were only in their boxers and lying too close for it to be anything but intimate.

"So they are…" words failed her.

"Bisexual, sleeping together," Heather nodded. "They have girlfriends occasionally but are each other's longest-running relationship."

"Oh wow," Erin muttered.

"I would have told you from day one," Heather said, "but Jody wanted to see what Rafi's end game was while pursuing you."

Erin looked down at the video. Rafi was running his

fingers through his hair agitatedly.

"I don't think Erin is desperately in love with me. I don't feel she is panting to do anything I say. She wasn't even interested in the Chan diamond. She didn't even comment on it once. Do you know how many women would die to just try on that ring? They would be talking about it every second they get."

"Give it time," Rich said drolly. "Who can resist your handsome face and the copious amounts of money you have at your disposal."

"I don't know," Rafi said fretfully, "I hate that Dad fired Suzette. Now she had the kind of devotion that would be handy for this kind of situation."

Rich visibly shuddered. "Suzette was a raging lunatic. 'I would do anything for you, Rafi; I'd kill for you, Rafi. I'd walk on glass barefoot for you, Rafi.'"

"And she was effective. I need a raging lunatic," Rafi said. "At least if she is caught poisoning my father, then we could just send her to a mental institution like they did Suzette."

"I don't want to talk about killing your father," Rich said, turning his back. "I want plausible deniability if things go sideways. Why don't you let the old man die naturally; he has cancer."

"It's in remission," Rafi snorted, "a miracle of miracles; the low doses of arsenic that Suzette was giving the old man actually cured his cancer. Why do these things only happen to me?"

Rich chuckled. "So you cured him. Why choose poison again this time?"

"You have a point," Rafi said contemplatively.

"I am not giving you any ideas," Rich said, "forget I said anything. This is the one thing I don't get about you. I could never see myself plotting to kill my father. I love my old man to pieces."

"We have two very different fathers," Rafi said, "your father leaves you alone to live your life; he doesn't care who you marry or if you marry. He knows what we get up to together and doesn't treat me any differently. If my father knew, he'd kill me, point blank." Rafi sighed. "I am just trying to get ahead of this and kill him first."

Erin looked up from the video and gasped. "I can't face him after this. This is madness!"

"I know," Heather said, "that's why I asked earlier if you know how to act."

"I don't," Erin said. "I am bad at it."

"Well then," Heather said, "write a letter to him, tell him goodbye, put your ring in it. And disappear."

"Disappear?" Erin asked. "I can't just disappear."

"There must be somewhere you can go until all of this blows over and Rafi finds a new patsy, someone willing to kill his father."

"I can't believe this," Erin muttered. "How am I going to know when he does that?"

"Check the news," Heather shrugged. "Anything the Chans do is news. Samir Chan dying will make the news, and Rafi Chan marrying will make the news."

"I can't just leave," Erin said. "Mr. Rogan hired me."

"Jody will tell Ralph why you left. Don't worry about it. Just get out of here and watch your back."

Erin did just that. She wrote a letter to Rafi, told him she had reconsidered and was sorry, booked her flight to Jamaica, and has been looking over her shoulder ever since.

Chapter Six

"**W**hy are we meeting so early?" Garwin asked Gersham grumpily. "It's barely five-thirty."

They were sitting in the seating area at the back of the restaurant, and Garwin still felt groggy. He had only fallen asleep in the wee hours of the morning after thinking about Erin for most of the night.

"We have a slew of things to discuss," Gersham said, "the adjoining event venue to the restaurant, Silver Manor, and this last-minute booking from Dennison and Associates."

"Okay," Garwin said, "hit me."

"The event venue," Gersham said, "Larry Nelson said it should take six weeks. I sent you the plan."

"When?" Garwin ran his hand through his hair.

"Last night," Gersham said. "I need your opinion."

"Haven't checked my phone." Garwin fished out his phone from his pocket and looked at the plan. It was pretty simple and straightforward, the same thing they had always discussed. Their dream was to have a venue with a separate entrance to the restaurant where they could host parties, weddings, receptions, and other large events. They had nearly a quarter acre of land to work with.

Larry had done a good job with the potential plan. He had made it both pretty and functional, the event hall seamlessly integrated with the landscaping outside. The inside was big enough to have a spacious dance floor, and the layout of the tables and seating arrangements had been carefully designed to ensure a smooth flow for both guests and staff.

Larry had also incorporated versatile design elements that allowed customization to suit different events.

The plan for the outdoor area was what Garwin was most interested in seeing. Larry had proposed a pergola, which would be perfect for hosting outdoor ceremonies or cocktail hours.

"Where's the water feature?" Garwin enlarged the picture on his phone. "I see the lawn area. Where's the fountain symbol?"

"There isn't one; I need to tell him to add that," Gersham murmured. "Are you okay with everything else, though?"

"Yup," Garwin nodded, "Larry's attention to detail is second to none. I like the location of the kitchen area, the restrooms, and the parking."

"All overflows can use this parking lot, of course," Gersham said. "I can't wait to see it come to life."

"You'll be going on your world tour," Garwin said, "you won't be around for it."

"I'll just be gone for three months," Gersham said, "do you think I'll be going away for longer than that?"

"No, sir," Garwin said. "But we both know that this is more your baby than mine. You won't rest easy knowing I am in charge of the project while you are gone."

"You are right," Gersham mused. "Do you want to come along on my tour?"

"As a third wheel to you and Patti? No thanks," Garwin said, "besides, who would run things here while both of us are gone."

"Erin," Gersham said, "she is quite capable of doing it."

Garwin smiled. "It wouldn't be right leaving her on her own."

Gersham chuckled. "I see."

"Now, if she could come with me, that would be perfect," Garwin murmured.

Gersham stared at him and shook his head. "I have never heard you talk like this about any girl."

"I don't know what's wrong with me," Garwin said. "I think she infected me with something."

"I think it's love," Gersham said. "You are finally in love."

"Nope, not love," Garwin shook his head. "I am just finally realizing the importance of having someone special to share life's adventures with—someone I can see myself hanging out with for the foreseeable future."

Gersham raised an eyebrow. "Sounds like love to me."

"Not every warm fuzzy feeling for a woman has to be labeled as love," Garwin said. "You know that song by Bryan Adams, 'I got no time for love, no mind for love…'"

"Why do you like that particular song so much?" Gersham frowned. "Of all Bryan Adams lovey-dovey songs, that's the one you memorized?"

"Yep," Garwin chuckled. "I have no time to love…no mind for love…"

Gersham cleared his throat dramatically. "I hear you. Now on to our next item…"

"I don't do love," Garwin said belligerently. "The sooner you acknowledge that, the better."

"I acknowledge that you think you are immune from love," Gersham grinned. "Can we talk about our next item of business?"

"Sure," Garwin nodded.

"Silver Manor," Gersham said. "Alison White from Denison and Associates sent this voicemail to me yesterday evening. As you know, I am acting as Dad's power of attorney, so all business related to the reinstatement of the will goes through me. Take a listen."

Gersham played the voice note.

"Hey, Gersham, this is Alison White from Dennison and Associates. I am calling to inform you that we have received the last will and testament of Fern Maria Silver from the police. It is now in our custody. In the original will, Sterling Silver and Joy Silver were given the estate to be shared equally between them. After an emergency hearing, the judge reinstated the original will. Sterling and Joy Silver are now the true owners of Silver Manor and the business previously known as Silver Chemicals.

Unfortunately, restitution takes a while. It will probably be a year or more before the business side of things gets sorted. Mr. Crook expanded Silver Chemicals to much more than it was before he stole it.

We will need time to secure your interests. In the meantime, the house will be available in three months. Apparently, Mr. Crooks was running it as a private bed and breakfast. It has bookings until the end of the year. You can decide whether you want to continue with the venture. We will look into how you can receive all the proceeds of the income generated from that property. Someone is occupying it now."

"Oh wow," Garwin muttered. "Have you told Dad and Aunt Joy?"

"Yes," Gersham said. "He was bawling inconsolably

when I did. His counselor said he is nowhere near ready to be out of the facility right now. When I told Aunt Joy, she was indifferent. She said when we visit, we should take pictures. She is too busy to come down here to check it out. So it's just me and you, kid."

"When we get the keys, we should go up there and celebrate."

"I don't know about that," Garwin said doubtfully.

"Come on, we have to," Gersham urged. "I have been dying to see what it looks like since we couldn't see it from the road. The way Dad describes it, it sounds like it is a beauty."

"He romanticized the place," Garwin said. "It's probably just an ordinary building. Did Leonard Crooks live there after he killed our grandmother for it?"

"I don't know," Gersham shrugged.

"Well, a little piece of me is curious, too," Garwin said. "Losing that house was one of the catalysts of our father's downward spiral into an unstable alcoholic. I want to see the stone and mortar that took him down."

Gersham nodded, "As soon as I get the keys, we go. Which brings me to my next item on the agenda."

"Morning, guys," Erin pushed the door open. "You are both here. I thought I was supposed to open up today."

"You were," Gersham said, "but I called an impromptu owners meeting. You are just in time for the segment of the meeting that will involve you."

Erin walked over. Garwin watched her advance. She wore the same outfit she had always worn: jeans and a polo top. Why was it he felt like quoting poetry? Today, her hair was slightly different. She wore a side part, her hair looked glossier than normal, and the red streak in her hair looked even deeper red.

"I have been meaning to ask, Erin," he said lazily, "why do you have a red streak in your hair?"

Erin laughed. "It's to color the white patch of hair I have right there. I was born with it. The condition is called poliosis. There is a lack of pigmentation in those follicles, so it's white. My Dad and my brother have it, too."

"Cool," Garwin grinned. "Just like Rogue in the X-men. Why can't I remember you with that in high school?"

"I've been coloring it since the second year," Erin sat down. "I used to be self-conscious about it."

"It would have made you stand out," Garwin said.

"Oh, it did," Erin chuckled. "My first year, they called me Miss Gray, Grandma. I couldn't bear the teasing, so I gave in and started dying it black with my grandma's box dye."

"Too bad," Gersham said. "If Garwin knew you had that feature, he would have followed you around like a puppy. Rogue was one of his favorite X-Men characters."

"It's true," Garwin chuckled. "I used to like Cipher too. I wanted her powers when my Dad came home drunk."

"Oh, because Cipher had the power of invisibility," Erin nodded. "I was partial to Storm myself. I loved the romance between her and Black Panther. Wakanda forever."

Gersham groaned, "Okay, nerds, can we get back to business?"

"Sure," Garwin leaned forward. "We have to discuss this some more, Erin."

"I'll add it to my list," Erin smiled. "We seem to have a lot of things in common."

"So, we were asked to cater the Dennison and Associates staff party at the end of the week. Their regular caterers bailed on them," Gersham said. "Allison said it was unexpected, so she begged me to take it on. I would have said no; it's short notice, but I feel obligated. They are our lawyers."

"The theme of the party is Nigerian Jamaican fusion. Dennison senior is Nigerian. This year, they want to celebrate the fusion of the two cultures."

"I know a bit about Nigerian food," Erin said. "I have done jollof rice before. I got compliments. Apparently, there is a difference in rice used between Nigeria and Ghana. If you want authentic Nigerian jollof rice, use long grain, not basmati."

"Noted," Gersham nodded. "And what else do you have experience with?"

"Pepper soup, using goat as the meat. It's kind of like our mannish water but spicier, way spicier," Erin said.

"And you, Garwin?" Gersham asked.

"I'll have to look up Nigerian cuisine online," Garwin chuckled. "But I am sure we can create a spread to get the theme right. Is it buffet style?"

"Yes," Gersham nodded. "I'll devise a menu later, and we'll divvy up the tasks. We meet back here at the end of the day. Maybe we can do some of the dishes as daily specials and get feedback in the meantime."

"Sounds like a plan," Erin jumped up. "I am running a little late."

"We'll meet later today," Gersham called after her retreating back.

Then he looked at Garwin skeptically, "I smell a romance brewing between you two. Please don't let it affect the work here. I don't want Erin to leave."

Garwin nodded. "I don't want her to leave either. The thought actually makes me feel nauseous."

"You are definitely in the throes of love," Gersham got up. "Or some powerful infatuation. Whatever it is, don't hurt Erin."

Chapter Seven

"**I**'ll drive you home," Garwin offered Erin after their meeting to finalize the menu.

"I'll close up this evening," Gersham said. "I appreciate you both going the extra mile for the weekend. And Erin, thank you for taking the lead on this."

"No problem," Erin nodded. "I am actually looking forward to the challenge."

She turned to Garwin, "Thank you for the offer of driving me home. I was wondering if I had the energy to walk up that hill tonight."

"Let's go," Garwin smiled. "It's not that late, you know. It's after six."

They headed for the bus in the nearly full parking lot. Garwin saw a hibiscus in full bloom and resisted the urge to pick one and hand it to her. What was wrong with him? He was short-circuiting, that was what. And he didn't want to stop; he liked the feeling. He wanted to see more of her and be in her presence.

"I was wondering if you wanted us to hang out somewhere. Do you realize we don't see each other outside the restaurant?" Garwin asked.

"I spent nearly all of today with you," Erin said. "I would think you would be tired of seeing me by now."

"And yet, I am not," Garwin said. "I think I have a slow-growing Erin addiction."

Erin smiled. "Well, I am not looking forward to going home tonight. So maybe I will take you up on your offer."

"Why?" Garwin opened the bus door and waited for her to get in. "What's going on?"

"My cousin Serena is moving in with her three munchkins," Erin sighed. "I just have a feeling that chaos is about to ensue."

Garwin nodded. "How old are they?"

"Eight, and five-year-old twins," Erin sighed. "And they are not the quiet stay-in-the-corner-and-play-with-your-dolls kind of children. Serena allows them to run amok while she pretends as if she doesn't hear them tearing down the place around her."

Garwin chuckled. "I have a four-year-old nephew; he's a handful too."

"Oh yes," Erin nodded. "Garnet had a baby. Where does he stay when she is on the cruise ship?"

"With my aunt Joy," Garwin walked to the driver's side. "So where would we go?"

"I have no clue," Erin said. "I don't want to go to a restaurant after spending all day in one."

"We can't go to a bar because I avoid them like the plague," Garwin murmured. "Do you drink?"

"Rarely," Erin said. "Maybe a toast at a wedding or a light beer now and again. I am a casual drinker, never been drunk."

"Good," Garwin nodded. "My father has ensured that I am a complete teetotaler. I have never had the desire to even touch a drink. I hate the scent of alcohol."

"Bad childhood memories?" Erin turned to him.

"The worst," Garwin said. "Sometimes I marvel that I am not even more messed up than I am today. I turned out to be pretty ordinary, maybe a little boring."

Erin laughed. "I have never been bored around you. You are quite entertaining, the life of the party, always cracking jokes and making people laugh. The staff in the kitchen adore you."

"It's a conscious decision I make," Garwin grinned. "I decide to be upbeat every day. I work hard at keeping my energy up and having a positive attitude because there was so much negativity around me while growing up. My football coach, Leyland Cole, was the one who drilled it into me: 'Garwin, you have to fight the negative with the positive. Don't let the darkness and dark thoughts swallow you.'"

"I started practicing it every time I felt dragged down into the depths of my dark wanderings. I think about something positive and uplifting. I think about the end of the bad situation. I change my reality with just my thoughts."

"Oh," Erin swallowed. "Well, that's a perspective I don't hear regularly."

"Gersham's therapist has him practicing mindfulness; it's the same thing," Garwin said. "I just got my advice for free when I was twelve and joined the football team."

"I see," Erin said. "It's incredible how such simple advice can shape a person's mindset. I've come to believe that our thoughts have immense power over our experiences, and it's up to us to harness that power for the better. I had a really nice coworker tell me that. She said she wrote daily affirmations on Post-it notes and read them every day. I thought it was cute until I got into a difficult situation the other day where I told myself all kinds of negative stuff and decided to follow her. So, I post my daily affirmations on the mirror. My grandmother calls them graffiti."

Garwin smiled. "What was your affirmation for today?"

"I am likable, lovable, and worthy of love," Erin said. "I know it sounds basic."

"No, it's good. It's a good one, and I agree," Garwin nodded. "Do you like jazz?"

"I don't hate it," Erin said.

"Good enough answer because I am determined that we go somewhere other than the parking lot of Silver Spoon restaurant," Garwin said. "My uncle Rufus and his band play at the Beach Hut on a Wednesday night."

"The Beach Hut?" Erin raised her brow.

"It's a place by the sea, rustic, classy, perfect for a low-key date, and we don't have to go home and change. We could listen to some jazz, eat an ice cream sundae, and even go and sit by the sea wall and chat."

"Sounds fun," Erin nodded.

****

The Beach Hut was indeed rustic, a round thatch-roofed place with weathered wooden walls that seemed to have absorbed the stories of countless seaside sunsets. The scent of salt hung in the breeze, and the soothing sounds of jazz music wafted in the air. There were four older gentlemen in the jazz band.

"What's their name?" Erin asked Garwin; she was fascinated with them. They wore formal clothes and felt hats, a throwback to a time gone by.

"Smoke and Silver Jazz Band," Garwin said. "Jefferey Smoke is the one on the piano, Rufus Silver is the one playing the saxophone, and the other two are Miles Drummond on the double bass and Charlie Keys on the trumpet. They've been playing together for years."

"'Smoke and Silver' is such a cool name. How did they end up together?"

"Jefferey and Rufus are childhood friends who grew up in Crimson Hills. They used to play in local clubs and bars in the sixties and then migrated to the UK. They both decided to return home to retire, found their old bandmates, and voila, they are back together again."

"They sound good," Erin relaxed in her chair. 'This is nice; it's like being transported to a different era.'

They ordered ice cream sundaes and chatted. Erin recognized some of the songs. She knew 'Unforgettable' by Nat King Cole. Rufus even serenaded the ladies with his version of Louis Armstrong's 'What a Wonderful World.' She found herself singing along.

She was enjoying herself; the combination of the rustic beach setting, the timeless tunes, and the band's camaraderie created a unique experience. She couldn't remember having so much fun in her life. Garwin was the perfect date. He was relaxed and charming and listened to her when she spoke. He was interested in her as a person. He was interested in her opinions.

They took a stroll on the beach; the further they walked, the more the sound of the jazz band faded, and the water lapping against the shore provided the music.

"What do you dream about?" Garwin asked Erin. "What do you ultimately want to do?"

"I don't know," Erin said contemplatively. "If you had

asked me this a year ago, I would have said I want to own a restaurant. I want to make the perfect chili sauce, can it, and sell it. I want to come up with a dish that is named after me. I might even have told you that I want to meet a handsome prince charming type of guy that will sweep me off my feet, will love me to bits, and has the means to take me to Paris on a whim."

"And now, today?"

"Today, I am running from Prince Charming; his charm was a lie. He was only dating me because I am a chef; he wanted someone who loved him without reserve and would do his bidding."

"Do his bidding?" Garwin raised an eyebrow. "That sounds old-fashioned."

"Their family is old-fashioned," Erin said bitterly. "And I want nothing to do with them. So I broke up with Rafi, and I am waiting until he has moved on before I can show my face in the light again."

Garwin stopped walking. "It's crazy; I assumed he wouldn't even consider you to be his wife because you are not an Indian girl from India or from a particular family. I thought that was how they did things."

"I heard that after Rafi proposed," Erin shrugged. "Maybe he had more leeway to do what he wanted."

"Come to think about it," Garwin said, "I should dislike Samir Chan too; wasn't he indirectly responsible for my mother's death? Depends on who you talk to. But I don't; it's hard to drum up negative or positive feelings for these strangers with whom I share DNA."

"Quite understandable," Erin said. "So tell me about you; what do you dream about? What do you ultimately want to do?"

"Mmm, let's see," Garwin said. "Being a chef is so time-consuming; I haven't thought about doing anything else, and business is booming, as you know. It would be nice to travel the world like Garnet and taste different cuisines. Sometimes, Garnet sends me videos of what she eats in different places, and I get envious. Maybe I could be a cruise ship singer like her."

Erin chuckled. "You sing?"

"I do," Garwin said. "The whole family on the Silver side is musical. We all had to learn to play a musical instrument when we were growing up; Aunt Joy insisted on it. I took piano lessons with Everton Murray, one of the best instrumentalists around up at the Nelsons house."

"I know," Erin smiled, "I remember Mercedes complaining that she had piano lessons with you on Mondays and Wednesdays. And I was so envious. I was like she has access to you, and she is complaining. Why couldn't it be me?"

"I am actually happy it wasn't you," Garwin held her hand, "maybe I would view you as a sister then. Just like I view Mercedes now. So this, you and me, would not happen in the present."

"Or maybe it would," Erin smiled, "we'll never know."

Chapter Eight

"**F**ound her." Hal Portman plunked down a brown envelope in his lap through the car window.

Rafi jumped. "What on earth?"

Hal chuckled. "Sorry, I am stealthy and efficient."

"And yet it took you six months to find Erin," Rafi hissed.

Hal walked around to the passenger side of the car. Rafi unlocked the door, and he got in.

"I had other things working on. I am a one-man operation. It's gonna rain," Hal said.

"I can see that," Rafi ripped open the envelope. "Where did you find her?"

"At a place called Crimson Hills," Hal said. "It was totally by chance, though. I was sitting in the parking lot at the Beach Hut, which is a little place by the sea, a really nice place. They have live jazz on Wednesdays, and there she was in the parking lot with a guy who looks a lot like you. She was smiling at him, giving him this soft, dewy look of love."

"Shut up," Rafi growled.

Hal nodded.

"Keep talking," Rafi said in exasperation. "I meant shut up about the dewy look of love business. Obviously, I want to hear more."

"Okay," Hal grinned. "The guy is Garwin Silver."

"I know about the Silvers. My nana Amita won't shut up about them."

"The second son looks like you," Hal said.

"I can see that," Rafi pulled out the photo of Garwin and Erin smiling at each other. "We both look like our grandfather."

"I remember your grandfather," Hal said, "he was a good man."

"He was just like my father. I would call him old-fashioned and unyielding, not good," Rafi murmured, "how ironic is it that Erin ran away to the same place my aunt Anya went to hide when she was running from her father."

"Oh yes," Hal said, "never saw the irony in that. Crimson Hill is like a refuge; it's the perfect place to lay low. They are a close community. When you ask questions, they clam up and look at you suspiciously. I had to follow Erin this past week to glean any information on her, and then I hit the jackpot. I started sweet-talking her cousin Serena and spent a pretty penny on her and her kids. Now, the woman thinks we are in a relationship. I am going to need extra money for Serena's shopping spree. That's in the expense report."

"Summarize it for me; I have a meeting with my father in ten minutes," Rafi said. "I think he found me a new bride or something. He sounded so pleasant over the phone; he is never this pleasant unless he found me someone to marry."

Hal chuckled. "So, I can anticipate that when he tells you

who it is, you will tell me her name, I pay her off, or turn her against you."

Rafi nodded. "Definitely stand by."

"Your father made three arranged marriages slip by, but he was dying at the time. He is not dying now; this one is going to be tougher for you to navigate with him not at death's door and distracted."

Rafi sighed. "So what is your suggestion? You are the one who arranged for me to poison him in the first place to hasten him along to death's door, and in the process, you cured him. Are you sure you are not working with my father?"

Hal snorted in laughter.

Rafi glared at him; it was not a trivial question.

"If he paid me more, I would work with him," Hal said. "I do gravitate to the highest bidder."

Rafi glared at him. "You are not loyal at all, and it bothers me."

Hal was in his late forties, built like a boxer. He had a high forehead, level brows, a hawkish nose, close-cropped curly hair, and medium-brown skin. Hal's mother had been Samir's housekeeper for years until she was fired from the latest cleansing of the staff.

He was a former policeman who had gone into private detective work nearly twenty years ago. He did steady work for the family through the years. It wasn't impossible that he could be playing all sides."

"What's next?" Rafi asked, irritated. "You are the ideas man."

"Find Erin," Hal said, "and marry her; she already has your ring."

"She left me," Rafi said, "and hid from me for six months. I do believe she probably hates my guts."

"You may be right," Hal murmured, "she has that copy

of your little confession while in bed with Rich Rogan. But think about it; she hasn't gone to the press or your father with it. She hasn't tried to blackmail you or anything like that."

"She just wants to forget me and took my family ring as payment," Rafi sighed. "I wouldn't mind forgetting her, but she has that video and my ring! I would like nothing more than to forget Erin, but that ring is a Chan family heirloom worth millions."

"Why did you give it to her in the first place?" Hal snorted. "You didn't want to marry her for real; why not give her an expensive diamond that doesn't have family sentiments attached?"

"My father had just given the pair to me in anticipation of my marriage to Chara. I had it on me, so I used it."

"Ah, Chara, she was so easy to pay off; she didn't want to marry you either," Hal grinned. "These young women these days, even in the depths of the villages where your father is digging them up from, they want a different way of life from the traditional; the elders should take note."

Rafi sighed. "We are talking about Erin; I want back that ring before my dad realizes it's missing. He'll probably ask about it when I see him today."

"I'll get it back," Hal said, "too bad Erin didn't want a lavender marriage or to be a stand-in chef for you to finish off your father. She would have been perfect for you."

"It wouldn't have been a lavender marriage," Rafi said, "I would have been committed to her. I would have stopped seeing Rich in that way; I would have married her after she killed my old man."

Hal laughed. "I don't believe that."

"Believe it," Rafi said, "when I am all in with a relationship, I go all in. I want to choose who I go all in with, not my father."

"Why don't you just hire a hitman and get rid of your father?"

"Too messy and too murderous somehow," Rafi said, "I don't like to think of myself as the kind of guy who would hire a hitman to get rid of a member of my family. The thought repels me. A little part of me is actually relieved that my father is still alive after the poisoning. I am not a monster like my father. I just want him out of my life and the Chan millions to do with as I would like."

"You really are a better man than your father," Hal nodded. "I've done things for him. If he wanted you dead, he wouldn't have been subtle about it. He would just hire a hitman. I think he would have you killed in a heartbeat if he ever found out that you are bisexual. Good thing for you. He usually asks me to set up his dirty deeds so I can give you a heads up."

Rafi sighed, "Thanks, I guess. What am I going to do, Hal?"

"Visit Erin, convince her to delete the video, and then ask her to marry you," Hal smiled. "She really is a lovely girl and quite pretty; she reminds me of a young Toni Braxton on the cover of her first album. Man, I had a thing for Toni; remember the song, 'Seven Whole Days,' and 'Breathe Again'?"

"I was born in the mid-nineties, Hal," Rafi said. "I don't even know those songs."

"You are a philistine," Hal snorted. "You young people are all philistines."

Rafi chuckled. "You mean philistine as in a person who is indifferent to culture and the arts?"

"Yes," Hal nodded.

"I am not indifferent; I grew up in a different era. Besides,

I never liked R&B much. I prefer reggae over R&B, Damian Junior Gong Marley over Bob Marley."

"I can't listen to this," Hal shook his head. "The blasphemous things you say."

Rafi grinned. "Hal, we are veering off-topic here. We are discussing Erin and the ring and the fact that you think she would marry me. What gives you that idea? Did her cousin say something?"

"No," Hal said, "she doesn't mention you at all. Her cousin knows nothing, but I thought it was worth a shot. She has the ring already. She obviously has a type. Make her choose between you and Garwin Silver. You are far richer and have more to offer than a mere chef in the corner of some backwater town."

"Sometimes it's not all about money," Rafi sighed. "Tell you what, you find the phone that she got the video on and take it to me. I'll delete it. Then, I'll approach her; I'll work my charm. I don't know if I have enough charm to get Erin to look at me favorably again. In any case, I need that ring back."

"I have to go; my father hates when I am late."

****

Samir's office was on the top floor of one of the newest buildings in midtown Kingston. Rafi hurried past the gigantic sign that read The Chan Group of Companies and into the elevator. His father did not like tardiness. He had lingered too long in the parking lot with Hal.

"You are late. He is expecting you," the secretary, Rebecca Dowel, growled.

Rafi smiled, but the smile did not reach his eyes.

His first order of business when he took over the group of

companies was to fire Rebecca Dowel. The woman treated him like a two-year-old boy instead of one of the VPs, and he knew that was because of his father.

She was Samir's mistress, an attractive woman in her late forties; she knew she was closer to Samir than everyone, including his family, and since his illness had progressed, she had established herself as a gatekeeper.

Even his mother had a tough time getting access to Samir these days. His parents had been living separate lives for years. His mother ran her own spice shop, lived on another wing of the house with her own entrance and staff, and generally minded her business.

They only came together as a family when they took traditional family photos. It was ironic they were far from a traditional family, and Samir was not a family man; he usually changed his mistresses every few years, sometimes he kept two at a time, and sometimes, like now, he had one.

Not one of them was ever Indian. His father tastes in mistresses was quite specific; they had to be curvy dark-skinned black women. That was his preference. They all knew this. It was the elephant in the room.

It baffled Rafi that his father did not follow the rules, so why was he continuing importing brides from India and keeping up with family traditions? Rafi had counted at least three half-Indian children who could be his siblings through the years. They were never acknowledged as Samir's, but he paid for their upkeep.

Rafi twisted his mouth. Samir's last will and testimony will be interesting, or maybe he would have it sealed like royalty. As if the whole world didn't know that the Chan family was not what they seemed. The forced smiles and unhappiness behind every eye can be seen in every photo they had out there. Samir was the only one living exactly as he wanted; everybody else had to suffer.

Rafi pushed the door into the inner sanctum. Samir was sitting at his desk, a newspaper opened in front of him. "Have a seat," he looked up. Rafi sat down in the plush office chair in front of him. He was looking good, way better than he had been in months. The cancer really was in intermission. His face was fuller, and his hair had grown back into lush, silvery waves. The bags under his eyes had reduced significantly. Even his complexion, which had taken on an ashen cast, now had a slight glow. The weight loss from the illness looked good on him. The man was flourishing.

"You look good," Rafi said grudgingly.

"Thank you," Samir nodded. "Did you see this article?" Samir pointed at the newspaper.

"I haven't had the time to read," Rafi said, "I just wrapped up our project with the St Lucian government."

Samir grunted, "It says: 'Every family has secrets, little pockets of information that for some reason or the other they are not willing to share with the world or even family members. A lifetime of deception can affect the bonds that hold a family together.'"

"Sounds like us," Rafi said.

Samir glared at him and then continued. "Anya Chan, my mother-in-law, was a woman of mystery and determination. When she was eighteen, she left the Chan family home in Montego Bay, Jamaica, taking refuge in the secluded Crimson Hills. There, she assumed a new identity, becoming known as Tina Boyd. It was in Crimson Hills that she crossed paths with Sterling Silver, former managing director of Silver Chemicals, who had lost his family business to the nefarious machinations of Leonard Crooks. Unfortunately, Sterling was broken by his loss and drank alcohol to soothe his pain."

"Oh my God," Rafi leaned forward. "Crimson Hills. Aunt Anya. Who was brave enough to write this?"

"Her daughter-in-law, Patti Sue Rafferty Silver," Samir said, "Normally I would leave this alone, but hearing this part is giving me pause— "Anya had hoped that her father and brother, known for their strict traditional values, would never find out about her new life. Samir Chan, Anya's brother and the head of the Chan dynasty, was furious. He ordered his security to bring Anya home. In the process, they intercepted a fight between Sterling and Anya. The situation escalated quickly; Anya fell and hit her head, and the security took her away from the premises and brought her home to Montego Bay. She was treated by a doctor, but it was too late. Anya had lost too much blood while her brother Samir considered how best to punish her for her infractions against the family."

"She is accusing me of murder," Samir leaned back in his chair. "I can't let this go."

"What are you going to do? Kill her in reprisal?" Rafi raised an eyebrow.

"I don't go around trying to kill people," Samir sneered, "unlike you."

Rafi gasped.

"I merely wanted to get her fired. Sue the paper, perhaps. But she is a freelancer and doesn't have a permanent job. I could punish her husband instead."

"Leave them alone; you took their mother from them," Rafi said heatedly. "There is nothing that you just read that was false! Nana Amita said you caused Anya to die!"

"My stepmother is fanciful," Samir said dismissively. "Anya was dead when she reached my home. If my men were not there to rescue her from that buffoon she was living with, she would have died anyway. It is quite rich to be blaming me when she was the one who was in an abusive relationship with an alcoholic."

"If you weren't such a stickler for tradition, she would have come home. She wouldn't have run away," Rafi said earnestly.

"Maybe," Samir steepled his fingers. "The past is gone; we can play the maybe game for a while, but the facts are that I should not be blamed for her injury or subsequent death. I called the paper and told them to remove the article from their website.

"Patti Sue Rafferty will not be doing part two. I can't do anything about the already printed paper, but it didn't cause an uproar; many people didn't read it. It is already yesterday's news. Now, as for you, I don't know if I should thank you or strangle you."

"Why?" Rafi asked nervously.

"You tried to kill me, and yet you cured me," Samir chuckled. "I both admire and fear you right now. I was curious about my cure. People rarely come back from my type of cancer. Then my doctor tells me, "Someone has been poisoning you secretly, Mr. Chan, with small doses of arsenic at just the right amount that actually killed the cancer cells. I wouldn't mind knowing what the exact dose was. Could you find out?"

"So I went searching for my potential killer, and wouldn't you know it, it turned out to be you."

"I…" Rafi swallowed.

"No need to give me excuses; I was determined to find out who did it. I eventually talked with Ralph Rogan, who put me on to his wife, who showed me the video; I had her destroy it. An employee of theirs said that only one other person had seen it. She sent a copy to one Erin McMillan, your so-called fiancée," Samir continued.

Rafi swallowed.

"You know, in the past," Samir said contemplatively, "I have thought about killing my own father, too. They were just fleeting thoughts; he was a hard-headed, pig-headed, stubborn brute of a man, but I would never have done it. What do you call it when you kill your father?"

"Patricide," Rafi swallowed. His heart was beating unevenly; he was waiting for his father to make a move, beckoning for someone to come out of the inner office with guns drawn or something.

"Patricide," Samir repeated, "and the killing of one's own son, filicide. You look scared, Rafi."

"I am," Rafi cleared his throat. "You are not exactly a warm, forgiving sort of person."

"No need to be scared," Samir rested back in his chair, "you inadvertently gave me a couple more years, according to my doctors; I am feeling generous and reflective."

"You are?" Rafi whispered.

"I am," Samir nodded. "I am not blind, Rafi. I know all of my immediate family hates me. I wondered which one of you was poisoning me at first. Imagine that a man could not be sure which one closest to him wanted him gone.

"I wondered if it was my wife, and then I concluded that she didn't hate me that much; she has her own life, her friends, her charities, and she has little time to want to kill me. We never really melded, Raya and I; she did her duty and bore me children. We never quite fulfilled the fantasy of falling in love after an arranged marriage."

Rafi nodded. His mother's regular mantra was that she didn't feel anything for Samir, whether good or bad.

"As for you, my firstborn, we never got along. It's as if you took one look at me at birth and decided that I wasn't to your liking. I must confess it came as no surprise when I watched you on the tape with your male lover, talking about my death, discussing ways to finish me off."

"Rich did not discuss finishing you off," Rafi said.

"I know, he wanted plausible deniability; I watched the video," Samir mused, "he loves his father. What does that feel like, loving one's father?"

"I have no clue," Rafi said frankly. "Our family does not do love. We do duty and tradition, judgment, and punishment. It is the Chan way or the highway, no love, no mercy."

Samir nodded. "You are right, and maybe that's why I am baffled. I don't know what to do with you, Rafi. Despite everything, I feel affection towards you."

"Let me live my life as I want," Rafi said earnestly. "You get to live yours! You have your mistresses, your outside children; you are a hypocrite, we all see it. Why pretend that you are a stickler for traditions? We know you are not; you are just enforcing an archaic way of doing things on your family. We all hate it and hate you for it. Did you know that Nikhil is in love with someone but can't commit because he knows you will arrange a marriage for him? Bela wants to be a lawyer and not some old man from India's wife."

"Enough!" Samir growled. "You win!"

Rafi stared at his father, stunned. "What?"

"You win," Samir said tiredly. "I tried to be like my father; I have no idea why. I never liked the man. Live your life, Rafi; I just have some conditions."

"What?" Rafi could scarcely believe what he was hearing; does this include a bride from India?

"No," Samir gritted. "I know you have been paying them off. Marry whoever you want. Of course, I'll run a thorough background check on her, and she has to be beyond reproach. The family business stays in the family, and that means grandchildren. I will not accept a relationship with you and another man."

Rafi nodded. "I accept that. I am not gay; I am…"

"We are not having this conversation," Samir growled. "I haven't changed that much."

Rafi nodded, "Okay."

"Good," Samir sighed, "please, try not to kill me again. I am grateful for the respite that I have now."

"I won't try to kill you again, father," Rafi whispered.

"Find and destroy the copy of the video that Erin McMillan has. If it ever gets out, I don't need to tell you how dangerous that video can be for our reputation. There is to be no newspaper article, internet video, or anything of that sort popping up like a bad sore and causing injury to the Chan name."

Rafi nodded.

"Don't mess this up, Rafi," Samir said, "if that video gets out, I will destroy Erin McMillan."

Rafi swallowed. "No need to go that far; Erin is not the kind of person to do blackmail."

"Let's hope so," Samir said, "you mentioned giving her a ring in your video with Rich…"

Rafi inhaled.

"Was it the Chan diamond?" Samir asked softly.

"It was," Rafi said.

"Where is it now?" Samir asked.

"She has it," Rafi said.

"Do you intend on marrying her still?" Samir asked.

"Well, no," Rafi said, "I doubt she will have me now after seeing the video; she fled St. Lucia and hid for a couple of months."

"Not my problem," Samir narrowed his eyes at Rafi. "How can you be so smart and stupid at the same time? You gave her a multimillion-dollar ring that's a family heirloom! Can I trust you with anything, Rafi?"

"I'll get it back," Rafi cleared his throat. "I know where she is; I will just find her and get it back."

"It's that simple, huh?" Samir sighed.

"Well, I just found her," Rafi said, "I'll get her to delete the video and give me back the ring. If she doesn't want to return it, I must convince her to marry me."

Samir laughed. "What a convoluted mess this is. I am giving you six weeks to sort this out, Rafi. If it's not sorted in six weeks I am going to have to get the ring back myself. Trust me when I tell you this: you do not want me to get involved."

Rafi swallowed. "I know. I'll sort it out."

Chapter Nine

Erin was seriously contemplating moving. It had been a week since Serena moved in, and the place was chaotic. She could barely move around the room; there were many bags and suitcases, and Serena was grossly untidy. Initially, Erin had scooped all of the clothes and knickknacks back onto Serena's bed, but Serena couldn't take a hint, and when she returned home, her bed was piled high.

"I met a guy, and I invited him over this evening," Serena said while Erin was pulling on her pants to go to work. "What time are you coming back home?"

Erin frowned. She knew her grandmother would not countenance any male visitors.

"So you just met a guy and are taking him to where you live already? He could be anybody!"

"But he's not just anybody; he's rich and interesting," Serena grinned. "He took me to a high-end restaurant and went shopping with me already. Some of these bags are from my shopping spree yesterday."

Erin snorted. "Ridiculous."

"You're just jealous that I can pull a rich man even after having three kids. I may not be able to get someone as handsome as Garwin Silver, but I still get my share of admirers. Wait, scrap that," Serena said, "I'm prettier than you. I bet if I made a serious attempt to fix myself up, I could get Garwin, too."

Erin gritted her teeth.

Ever since Garwin dropped her home three nights ago, Serena has had a bee in her bonnet about Erin and Garwin having a relationship. Serena apparently had a crush on Garwin; why else was she constantly comparing their looks?

Serena came and stood behind her. "What does Garwin see in you? You don't wear makeup; you do nothing to your hair."

"I thought you were talking about your new sugar daddy," Erin murmured.

Serena nodded. "Oh yes, Hal. He wants to see where I live."

"Good luck taking him over; Gan Gan will not allow male visitors if you're unmarried."

"I know," Serena said, "but she has choir practice tonight. When she's gone, he'll come over, and I'll sneak him out before she gets back. Hal wants to meet the kids."

Erin looked at her cousin skeptically. "You just met this man, and you're bringing him here to meet your children? Are you so desperate for male attention?"

"He bought them toys yesterday," Serena said, licking her lips and pouting in the mirror. "And I'm not desperate!"

Erin rolled her eyes. Serena still acted like a teenage girl, and without the makeup and wigs she liked so much, she looked like she did in high school—having toffee-colored skin still prone to acne and a heart-shaped face that retained a certain innocence.

Erin glared at her preening cousin. "Do not let him go near my bed. He's not supposed to sit on it, touch it, or go near my things."

"You've always acted like you're better than me, Erin, just because you went to college, had a fancy career as a chef, and didn't get pregnant in high school."

"Okay then," Erin chuckled, "your insecurities are showing."

"I'm not insecure," Serena narrowed her eyes, "why would I be? We're in the exact same space and situation. Granted, you do have a job, and I don't at the moment. But how are we different? You're here, living with Gan Gan again. In her little crappy guest room."

"I told you before," Erin said, "it didn't work out at my previous place of work. You should understand how that goes; you can't keep a job for three months."

"I have worked for more than three months!" Serena said, offended. "I worked for three months and four days at a clothing store in Trelawny."

Erin sighed; the insult had not connected.

"Don't think you can distract me," Serena said, "why are you back here? Your parents are wealthy; they live in a mansion in Cayman. Why are you here in Crimson Hills, Jamaica? Did you move back because of Garwin? I don't get it. Did you steal something? Were you fired?"

Erin sighed again. "Please, spare me; I don't want to discuss what happened."

"Mmm," Serena said, "I have been asking around, and no one in the family seems to know."

"Good," Erin said.

"All I know is that you used to work for Ralph Rogan in

St. Lucia. The Ralph Rogan, you were his personal chef. It had to pay well. What did you do to mess it up?" Serena sat at the edge of her bed and mused.

Erin pulled the brush through her hair a little harder than she would, hurrying to leave her querying cousin.

"You didn't have an affair; that's not your style," Serena mused. "You are probably still a virgin. Though how you could still be around all those wealthy men is weird. I would have bagged one by now; it's not as if you look half bad."

Erin chuckled. "Well, thank you, I guess."

"Have you met Rafi Chan?" Serena asked interestedly.

"Rafi Chan?" Erin asked weakly.

Serena nodded. "I saw a picture of him. He looks like Garwin Silver."

"Where did you see a picture of him?" Erin asked.

"Hal was reading some business magazine yesterday while waiting for me. I was shopping. Rafi Chan and his friend Rich Rogan were on the front page; they just finished a joint project in St. Lucia," Serena shrugged. "He was in St. Lucia; you were in St. Lucia. It doesn't take Sherlock Holmes to work out that you may have met him."

"I met him, yes," Erin nodded.

"And?" Serena raised her brows.

"And nothing," Erin said, "he likes roasted chicken. I was a chef at Ralph Rogan's place, an employee, not a guest."

"Oh," Serena said, disappointment in her voice. "I was hoping to hear more about Rafi Chan. Hal said he met him once at a business function; he is a very important man. If I had access to the Chans and Rogans of this world, I would be offering more than roast chicken."

Erin snickered. "You sound thirsty."

"If I had access to Rafi Chan, I would be his mistress at the drop of a hat," Serena said dreamily. "Can you imagine all of the traveling we would do, the gowns I would wear, the kind of life I would have?"

"Interestingly, you say mistress, not wife," Erin pointed out.

"I am being realistic," Serena laughed.

"Mama!" Serena's son, Travis, barged into the room without knocking; his two sisters, Tavia and Tala, followed.

Erin grabbed her bag to leave the room; it was about to get noisy when Serena's children woke up.

"No one goes on my bed," she warned the children sternly.

The two little girls looked at her, their eyes wide. They were so cute, with their little button noses and cupid-shaped lips. Erin's heart melted a little, but she knew that behind those pretty little faces was trouble.

The boy grinned slyly, probably planning to jump up and down on the bed with his dirty feet to spite her. He sometimes pretended he was deaf.

"Come on, my lovelies, let's get out of cousin Erin's hair," Serena said, "it's time to get ready for school."

Erin inhaled raggedly; she didn't know if she could take this one more morning. Three mornings were enough. She looked around for her phone. She usually kept it on the dresser, but today, it was overflowing with shopping bags courtesy of Serena and her new sugar daddy, Hal.

"Where is my phone?" she asked Serena as she exited the room with her children.

"How should I know?" Serena frowned.

"I usually keep my two phones on the dresser," Erin said in frustration, "I can remember placing them here last night when I got in."

"I am pretty sure it's in there somewhere," Serena said, "no need to sound so accusatory; I wouldn't take your phone; I have two of my own."

"I am not saying you took it," Erin gritted her teeth. "I have a couple of recipes saved for a Nigerian-themed party that I am catering for today. Now I can't find them."

"Isn't that a phone?" Serena pointed to the floor.

Erin looked down; there was her phone. The cheaper one, the one she had acquired when she had just moved back in with her grandmother. It was not the one with the incriminating video of Rafi and Rich in bed.

"Where's the other one?" Erin asked, exasperated.

"I'll find it for you today when I am organizing my stuff," Serena said, "it can't be far. Were you going to use it today?"

"No," Erin sighed. "I have important things on there. I can't afford to lose it."

"And it's not lost," Serena frowned, "trust me, I'll find it. By the time you get back later, it will be here, and the dresser will look nearly as neat as when I am not around."

****

"You have been frowning all day," Garwin said while they loaded the bus with food warmers. "I think you growled at me one time."

Gersham was going to oversee the office party for the afternoon.

"I wasn't conscious of it," Erin said, "I lost my phone."

Garwin looked at the phone she had clipped to her waist and raised his eyebrows.

"I mean the other one," Erin sighed, "my important one. The one I don't want to lose; it has important stuff on there."

"Ah," Garwin nodded. "I understand."

"I don't know if it is lost or if it's just mixed up in Serena's clutter. Did I tell you I am this close," Erin squeezed her fingers together, "to moving out."

Garwin nodded. "You did say that a couple of hundred times these past couple of days."

"I am seriously going house hunting," Erin said, "I cannot stay there a minute more."

"Nobody is staying at the Rafferty place," Gersham said behind her, "you are free to stay there if you want."

"Enid Rafferty's haunted house?" Erin frowned, "Patti used to complain about that place every day for all of our high school lives."

"It's only haunted if you can see into the spirit world like Patti," Gersham said, "have you ever seen a ghost?"

"No," Erin shook her head.

"Me neither; I slept over there many nights with Patti and never saw what Patti was talking about."

"It's the place for you," Gersham said, "five bedrooms and bathrooms filled with antique furniture, newly renovated in some places. If you see a ghost, just call for Garwin in the night."

"Are you serious about me staying there?" Erin asked.

"Yes, you can stay there until it's sold," Gersham said. "Patti and I are considering selling the place; neither of us wants it. Patti is not interested in any of the furniture. It's been months since Miss Enid passed, and she hasn't gone into Miss Enid's things to sort them out. Maybe with you living there, she will be brave enough to do it. We have to prep the place for sale, now is as good time as any."

"Okay," Erin nodded, "I'll live there."

"You sure?" Garwin asked doubtfully.

"How bad can it be?" Erin asked. "I prefer a haunted house to Serena."

"It's not bad at all," Gersham said. "Mira cleans it every two weeks, and I mow the lawn every month. I plan to ask Willie to take care of the yard when I'm not here. He used to do it until Miss Enid stopped paying him; that's when I took over."

Erin chuckled. "Okay, I'll move in tonight."

"I'll call Patti; she'll bring you the keys," Gersham said.

Garwin frowned. "Erin, are you sure you will be comfortable in that monster of a house?"

"Miss Enid used to live there alone," Erin pointed out.

"You have a point," Garwin nodded. "I could help you move tomorrow. Today, I will pick up my car in Montego Bay."

"Patti will help her move," Gersham said. "She has been asking me to follow her up to the house. I haven't gotten a chance to yet; now is a great time for her to visit with you around."

Chapter Ten

"**A**h, the famous Rafferty House, it's so pretty. It looks the same, just fresher," Erin said to Patti when they drove up the winding driveway and parked in front of the dark, imposing front door.

"That's the look we were going for," Patti whistled. "Did you know it was the second house built in Crimson Hills? My aunt bought it from one of the Wessons way back when. And you know they were the ones who owned all of the property up here."

"You may have mentioned that before; I can't remember. How old is it?" Erin got out of the car and stared at the house in awe. She always liked coming to Rafferty House.

"More than a hundred years old," Patti shrugged. "I can't remember exactly how much. Maud Beecher knows the history. Maybe the trustees at the Great House will want to repurchase it."

"And you have no attachment to the place?" Erin asked.

"It's an honest-to-goodness piece of history. It's still so pretty; look at all of the stones. It's a warm cream color. I love a house with gables and wood shingles."

"The wood shingles are now synthetic wood, faux cedar," Patti chuckled. "I had to change the whole thing a few months before Aunt Enid passed. The real cedar wood shingles lasted nearly fifty years."

"Oh wow," Erin murmured. "You went out of your way to preserve the authenticity. A little part of you must feel something for the property."

"Nope. I still have zero attachment to this place," Patti said. "I usually want to escape when I come here; it gives me the creeps."

Erin chuckled. "We should have a girls' get-together over here like in high school. You wanted us to sleep over all the time."

"Because I was scared out of my wits while here," Patti said. "I didn't want to sleep alone. Aunt Enid would be locked away in her suite of rooms while I am battling ghosts in my room."

"Were you really battling ghosts?" Erin asked.

"No," Patti said, "I didn't battle them; they didn't bother me, but still, I could see them, and that scared me for a long time."

"I never saw ghosts when I slept over here," Erin said, "I should be fine."

"Yes, you should." Patti opened the front door into a grand room. "I am the only one plagued by them, it seems. Let me give you a grand tour of all the changes made through the years since you were last here."

"I can't wait," Erin said excitedly.

"In here is the drawing room, otherwise known as our foyer and living room since we live in post-colonial days."

Erin chuckled. "It looks the same."

"Yep, all dark and dreary," Patti snorted, "let us open the windows, pull the curtains, and let in some light and fresh air. It smells like Aunt Enid's orange blossom potpourri."

"I like the scent," Erin said, heading for the patio doors and pulling the curtains.

"It smells like ghosts," Patti said.

Erin chuckled. "I see modern sliding doors."

"Yep, the old-school plantation-style doors added to the darkness. Gersham convinced my aunt to change them to glass. He paid for it himself."

Erin chuckled. "Did Aunt Enid pay for anything?"

"Not if she could help it," Patti laughed. "Even the furniture she never paid for; they came with the house, and she barely added anything new. I am going to sell it just like how she got it. I have to sort out her clothes and personal effects first, which shouldn't take long. I am so happy you are here as company."

"And I am happy for a place to escape Serena and my grandmother," Erin said.

"Which room will you choose?" Patti asked her after they toured the four ensuite bedrooms upstairs, each with their own balcony.

"Not your old room," Erin said, "to be safe. I don't want to see ghosts. Not in your aunt Enid's room either; that is too big for me. I think you could hold a football match in there; to me, it's still her room."

Patti nodded, "I know what you mean."

"I'll choose the black and white guest room; the blue one is too blue for me."

"Good choice," Patti said. "You can see both the road and a sliver of the sea across the trees from that room. Remember to pull your curtains at night; someone can watch you from the road at night."

"No one is interested in me like that," Erin chuckled.

"Not even Rafi?" Patti raised her eyebrows, "I thought you were hiding out here from him."

Erin opened her mouth and then closed it. "Not even him. How did you know we had a thing?"

"Are you going to tell me what happened?" Patti asked. "You told Garwin you didn't like his face; it had the poor guy concerned."

Erin grimaced. "It's a long story. I would rather not go into it."

"I understand wholeheartedly," Patti nodded. "They are not people to be messed with, apparently. Remember that article I wrote about the Chans?"

Erin nodded. "It was good."

"My friend Nora was the editor; she always likes the hard scoops. You should have seen the two of us as we anticipated the furor it would cause when people read it. Do you know what happened instead?"

Erin shook her head.

"Samir Chan happened," Patti seethed, "he got the owners involved; they have scoured all traces of it from the internet. They demoted Nora, and they got me blacklisted even from the other national papers."

"His lawyers sent me a nasty letter about slander and malicious spreading of information. Basically, part two of my article is dead in the water. I can't even defy them and put it up on the internet, or they'll sue. I bet they get away with murder all the time."

Erin gasped. "Do you seriously think they murder people?"

"Well, why not," Patti shrugged, "if they can murder people's careers because they just stated the bare facts, can you imagine if someone had real dirt on them? I imagine they would have no qualms in eliminating the offending person from existence."

Erin swallowed.

"Wait a minute," Patti looked at her stricken expression, "you don't have real dirt on the Chans, do you? Like evidence of Rafi doing something. Of course you do," Patti answered, "that's why you ran and are hiding out here. It makes sense."

"Well, I…" Erin stammered.

"Don't tell me," Patti widened her eyes. "I genuinely don't want to know what it is. If you tell me, I'll think about it and want to write a story about it. I'll want to tell the world what a strange family they are."

Erin nodded. "They are strange."

"Let's go get your things," Patti said, "and then I can tackle Aunt Enid's stuff. We can even make it a thing; I'll call Mercedes, she can come over. It will be like old times."

****

"Thank you, Patti, for inviting me over," Mercedes said. They were in the depths of Miss Enid's large walk-in closet, putting clothes into boxes. "Even though you are working me without pay."

"You can take whatever pieces of clothing you want from here," Patti said. "I will give the rest to Maud Beecher at the great house. She said she would dispose of them for me."

Erin giggled.

Mercedes rolled her eyes. "No thanks, I will eschew the pay. I am not into vintage clothing."

"She is still talking like a dictionary," Patti mumbled. "Who uses the word eschew in casual conversation? I don't even talk like that, and I am the writer."

Erin laughed. "What do you expect? Mercedes had elocution classes when she was twelve."

"Yep, there is a story behind that," Mercedes said. "My mother overheard me swearing and talking some really filthy stuff. Of course, it was all Larry's fault; he was teaching me swear words and slang from different cultures. We were just culturally curious, that's all."

"Yeah right," Erin chuckled.

"That's when she decided to send me and Larry to Dr. Bogle's elocution classes for the refined young person."

Patti laughed. "I remember those classes, Aunt Enid said she would have sent me if Dr. Bogle wasn't charging so much."

"I only knew about them because Garwin went to them," Erin chuckled. "I was very curious about his Saturday classes with Mercedes."

"My mother convinced Garwin's aunt to let him go because she overheard him swearing. Garwin swears to this day that he didn't swear, but my mother was paying for it, and it wasn't hurting him, so he had to go to the elocution classes."

Patti laughed. "Aunt Bunny should have just adopted Garwin and be done with it."

"She loves him dearly," Mercedes sighed, "and she is the reason why Larry, Garwin, and me have the same accent and will use random words like eschew in our speech. We had to enunciate and learn words for exactly one year. It was like spelling bee on hyper speed."

"What was it like growing up with Garwin?" Erin asked.

"You still have a crush on him?" Mercedes asked incredulously.

"And he has a huge one on her," Patti murmured. "But I don't think it would be called a crush at their age. I think they are in love."

"You are right. It's not a crush," Erin said dreamily. "I tried to harden my heart against him, and I was doing well for nearly six months, but I am smitten."

"Especially because you were predisposed to it from high school," Mercedes grinned. "I remember how you were. Garwin once came over to have lunch with us, and you didn't eat. You kept your head down and avoided looking him in the eye."

Erin laughed. "I was ridiculous."

"No, it's understandable," Mercedes said, "Garwin is quite handsome, polite, friendly, and easy to talk to. I might have been awestruck like you and Patti if I hadn't grown up around the Silver brothers. Isn't it amazing Patti got married to Gersham, and you are…"

Mercedes frowned, "What are you and Garwin to each other?"

"Talking, hanging out," Erin said. "I almost married a man who looks like him."

"You have to tell me more," Mercedes said.

"And while you two talk," Patti said, "could you please pack the clothes and put them in the boxes? Remember, this is a packing party, yay."

Mercedes and Erin laughed.

They made short work of it, chatting and laughing until they were done. After finishing, they lugged the boxes into Mercedes' SUV one by one.

"I am glad that's done," Patti said, "now onto Mercedes' mother-in-law we go. This just leaves Aunt Enid's papers and books. I'll just sell most of the books with the house. The personal unnecessary papers, I'll just burn them."

"Wait a minute," Erin frowned. "What do you mean Mercedes' mother-in-law? How is Maud Beecher related to

Mercedes' husband?"

"It's a long story," Mercedes said, "I'll tell you while we are on the way."

By the time they reached Crimson Hill Great House, just a three-minute drive, Mercedes had told her how she met Charles.

Erin sat in disbelief, staring at Maud when she came out to greet them.

"Erin," Maud came to the car door and smiled at her. "How are you, child? It has been too long."

"It has been," Erin cleared her throat loudly. "it's nice to see you, Maud.

"She's shocked," Mercedes chuckled, "I just told her about how I met Charles and your travels through time."

"Oh," Maud smiled.

"Do you see me when you time travel?" Erin asked Maud, point blank.

"Rarely, you don't come up here much in the future. I only see the people that visit here," Maud said, "your children do, though; they play with my grandchildren. You have a son who looks just like that pretty father of his. I mean a dead ringer for him. Anya Chan's face lives on to another generation."

Erin gasped.

"Maud," Mercedes said, a warning in her voice.

"I am married to Garwin?" Erin asked.

Maud smiled. "I have said too much already. Would you ladies like to come inside?"

"I have more stuff to go through, mostly papers," Patti said. "I will have to create a save pile, a donate pile, and a burn pile. This will take me a while."

"Yes! I want to come inside," Erin nodded. "I want to hear more about my children with Garwin."

"What I told you is all I am going to tell you," Maud said, "I said too much already; I will not say another word."

"And it was just a possible future anyway," Mercedes said, looking at the disappointment on Erin's face. "Cheer up, girl."

Chapter Eleven

It was late after Patti and Mercedes left. Erin had a shower in her spacious bathroom and luxuriated in the fact that she was in a big room with no Serena. She was feeling pretty after her extended shower, so she pulled on one of her newer sun dresses that she had bought in St. Lucia. It was yellow, sleeveless, and had an A-line cut, and she let out her hair. It felt good to take it out of her usual ponytail.

She examined it closer in the mirror; she needed a trim. It was inching down to her mid-back, and she didn't want it so long. She wanted to maintain it at shoulder length; it was much easier to manage that way. The women on her mother's side of the family were blessed with fast-growing hair. She felt a surge of nostalgia to see both of her parents.

She had skirted the issue of St. Lucia with her parents but she needed to call them to tell them that she had moved. Thankfully, they were too busy to probe into her business too closely. They had both been recently promoted in their respective jobs. Her father was a new VP at the bank where he worked, and her mother was made the head of IT at the bank where she worked.

She glanced at the clock; it was seven o'clock. They were probably still at work. She sent them a text instead to keep them in the loop because she was sure that her grandmother would not give them a report that would show her in a favorable light. Gan Gan was not pleased when she said she was moving out.

And then she remembered Serena was going to find her phone.

Serena would be at home. She dialed the number swiftly, almost breaking her nail.

"Did you find my phone?" Erin asked when Serena answered.

"No," Serena said, "couldn't find it. Why didn't you tell me you were moving out? You made me clean the room for nothing."

Erin frowned. She couldn't afford to lose the phone.

"Did you look everywhere?" She asked, "Under the bed? Did you check if it got mixed up with one of yours?"

"Checked everywhere," Serena said, "I even went to the living room and checked under settees. Are you sure you left it here?"

"Very sure," Erin sighed, "I don't take it to work. I had it in the top dresser drawer in a handbag. I took it out to charge it; I was talking to Gan Gan, got distracted, and went to work. When I returned, the room was packed with your things, and the next day, the phone was missing. It is hard to miss; it has a shiny gold case. If only it had a charge and was on, I could ring it."

"I didn't take it," Serena said petulantly.

"You said that already," Erin murmured.

"Gan Gan wouldn't take it either," Serena said, "she is not fond of cellphones, and she wouldn't know how to use your fancy smartphone. She is a old school phone kind of girl."

"She is the last person I suspect would think about taking it," Erin sighed. "I need to find it; I have important things on there."

Serena cleared her throat. "Do you know Hal?"

"Hal, the new guy who bought you many things?" Erin asked.

"Yes," Serena said.

"I have never met anybody named Hal," Erin said, "What's his surname?"

"Portman."

"Is Hal short for something?" Erin asked.

"Nope," Serena said. "Not according to him; he said his name was just Hal."

"Never met him, why do you ask?"

"He spent most of today grilling me about you and our family, but mostly you," Serena said. "At first, I didn't realize what was happening, but then I told him about your lost phone, and he was too interested. He even offered to look for it with me. He went through the closets and everywhere, double-checking things like it was important to him. It was bizarre."

"That is bizarre," Erin gasped. "What did you tell him about me?"

"I don't know anything much about you," Serena growled. "You don't tell me much. I don't know why you are back here or what you have gotten yourself mixed up with. Is he the police? Did he buy me all of those things because he wanted me to get chummy with him? I am such a pushover. I am going to get my life together."

"Serena," Erin said firmly. "What exactly did he ask you?"

"He was asking about your likes and dislikes, what you were like in high school, your relationship with Garwin Silver. I told him what I knew before I started getting suspicious. He was more interested in you than me. Come to think of it, he asked many questions about the Silvers, Gersham, Garwin, and Garnet. He wanted to know how Sterling Silver could afford such an expensive rehab. And he wanted to know about a video. He asked if you had ever shown me a video with Rafi Chan. Do you have a sex tape, Erin?"

"No, I don't," Erin inhaled. Rafi had found her. He probably found out about the video that Heather had sent her.

"Are you sure?" Serena asked.

"Of course, I am sure," Erin snorted. "What did Hal say his business was? And what is he doing in Crimson Hills?"

"He said he is a salesman," Serena whispered. "He is staying at Silver Manor. He said his boss had him rent it out for three months, and they had business here. Are you the business, Erin? Is he a hitman? Is he a private investigator? A reporter? The FBI? CIA? Mafia?"

The buzzer at the gate went off, and Erin jumped. "I am sure he isn't a hitman. He would have killed me already. It's not law enforcement; I didn't do anything wrong. I have to go; someone is at the gate."

"Wait!" Serena sounded genuinely terrified. "Don't hang up. Check who it is."

Erin dutifully got up and checked; she was nervous, too.

"It's Garwin," Erin exhaled in relief.

"Just got back from getting my new car," he said over the intercom. "Want to go for a drive?"

"It's Garwin," Erin said to Serena.

"Oh," Serena sighed. "At least you have him. Then again, by the looks of Hal, Garwin would lose in a fight."

"Thanks for the heads up about this, Hal Portman," Erin said.

"No problem," Serena said. "You were right; I was crazy for bringing a man I just met to the house. You know what gets me? He thought I was so dumb he could just ply me with gifts and that I would tell him everything about Crimson Hills. I may be a materialistic country bumpkin, but I am a smart country bumpkin. You be safe out there, Erin."

Chapter Twelve

"**W**ow," Garwin said when he saw her. "You look amazing. I have never seen you with your hair down."

Erin laughed and swung her hair a bit. "Oh, really now?"

"Really," Garwin breathed. "I like it."

"So, this is the new car," Erin said, dragging her eyes from the intensity in his.

"It is," Garwin said, "my first personal vehicle."

"It is nice," Erin said, "and it's in my favorite car color, dark grey."

"Yes, I remember you saying that," Garwin said, "that must be why I subconsciously chose it."

Erin laughed, "Sometimes I have to pinch myself that this is not a dream, Garwin Silver thinks about me."

"I do, very frequently," Garwin opened the passenger door, "Let's take this baby for a spin," Garwin said, "and go to Knightsbridge Farm. It's Jack's birthday party."

"I am not dressed for a party!" Erin squealed. "Besides,

I haven't seen those people in ages; I can't just show up looking basic."

"You are never basic, and you look pretty hot now. I fail to see how you can upgrade this look," Garwin looked at her from head to toe. "You are the most naturally beautiful woman I know. You don't need a lick of makeup to have me taking glances at you and wanting to write poetry."

Erin grinned. "Thank you."

"I mean it. I am not just saying these things," Garwin said.

Erin got into the car and inhaled. "I love the new car smell."

"Me too," Garwin said, "how was your moving in today? Went okay?"

"Yes, it did. Mercedes came over, and we helped Patti clean out her aunt's closets, and we delivered the stuff to Crimson Hill Great House. Maud Beecher said our children will play with Mercedes' children. She said one of our sons looks just like you."

Garwin laughed. "I see Maud is up to her usual prophesying."

"Do you believe her?" Erin asked. "Mercedes and Charles's meeting was pretty intense. It all came through."

Garwin shrugged. "I treat Maud's time traveling like I do astrologists, zodiac card readers, palm readers, and that kind of thing with a high dose of skepticism. In my opinion, even if they are right, knowing things beforehand is cheating; it takes the joy out of the journey."

Erin nodded. "I see what you mean."

"And on another note," Garwin smiled, "did you find your phone?"

"No," Erin sighed, "but I found out that Rafi Chan found me."

"What do you mean by Rafi Chan found you? Were you

hiding from him?"

"Not exactly," Erin said, "I am assuming he found out that I have the video of him plotting to use me to kill his father."

"Ah, I see," Garwin said.

"I think he wants to make sure it's gone. I was hoping he wouldn't find out I had a copy of the video," Erin sighed. "His private investigator wined and dined Serena and tried to inveigle information out of her."

"Did he succeed?" Garwin asked.

"I didn't tell her much of anything," Erin said, "so she wouldn't be able to say much."

"That's smart," Garwin frowned, "why did you keep the video though?"

"I was thinking of using it as leverage, just in case Rafi came after me," Erin said, "remember the man wanted to use me to commit murder?"

"Yes," Garwin nodded.

"And now my phone with the video is missing," Erin sighed.

"Oh," Garwin raised an eyebrow.

"I don't know where it is," Erin fretted. "My leverage over Rafi has vanished into thin air. I know the Chans are quite capable of bad things. Rafi is quite capable of bad things. I shouldn't have kept that stupid video. What if someone finds it?"

Garwin nodded. "I don't think anyone can just access your phone, right? Isn't it password-protected?"

"It is," Erin nodded.

"And it's not like Rafi Chan would hurt you before he made sure you deleted the video," Garwin said. "At the moment I doubt you have anything to worry about where he is concerned."

Erin nodded. "You are right."

Garwin squeezed her hand. "Everything will work out. I am sure your phone is not far."

Erin squeezed back, a shiver of desire working its way up her fingers and wrapping around her heart. Garwin's touch ignited a spark within her; their eyes met and held with a reassuring glint in his.

He leaned closer. "Whatever happens with this Rafi guy, I'll be right here with you, ready to face anything."

Erin felt her cheeks flush. The tension between them thickened. Garwin's touch had a powerful effect.

Garwin traced small circles on the back of Erin's hand with his thumb. "Ready to party?"

"Not really," Erin forced her mouth to move. Could a small, innocuous touch make your mind go numb? It was as if his intense gaze, filled with unspoken affection, held her captive. "I haven't seen or spoken to these people in ages."

"No worries," Garwin removed his hand from hers and started the car. "It will be as if you never left."

The intensity of the moment shattered. Erin exhaled in relief, trying to sound normal.

"Do you know that in high school, we used to call you, Jack Knight, Derrick, and Lee Wiley, the cute guy's crew?" Erin chuckled.

"Is that so?" Garwin laughed.

"Yup," Erin nodded. "We thought the conditions for acceptance in your little friends' group were that you had to be handsome."

Garwin laughed out loud. "Oh really?"

"Yes, really," Erin said. "Unsurprisingly, they are all married and are off the market. Mercedes gave me a rundown of all the couplings going on up here. Some of them I knew of, like Larry and Jill, Jack and Cambria, and some I definitely expected, like Derrick and Cindy and Lee and Dacy. But I hear Leighton and Camille hooked up, and Orandy and Nicky."

"Yup," Garwin nodded. "These days, hanging out with my friends is being the third wheel, but it's fine. I have you now."

"Are you saying that we are an official couple?" Erin smiled.

"Yes," Garwin said. He passed through the first security post at Knightsbridge farm; they verified his identity, and then he stopped. "I think we should seal it with a kiss."

He turned to Erin, and before she could think of what he would do next, he cupped her face in his hands and pressed his lips gently against hers.

The world seemed to fade away as the soft warmth of the kiss enveloped them. Erin's heart fluttered, and she melted into the moment, forgetting about the outside world.

She didn't want him to stop; she wanted him closer. So, this was what true sexual attraction felt like. Her girlhood years of imagining just this kind of scenario were coming through.

"Sealed with a kiss," Garwin said when they came up for air.

"Well, I guess that makes it official," Erin smiled.

Garwin chuckled, "I've wanted to do that for a while now. I just needed the perfect moment."

****

Jack Knight was exactly how Erin remembered him—tall, gangly, and cute. He had his hand draped around Cambria, his wife, with a drink in the other. He greeted them profusely when they got there.

"Garwin! Erin!"

Erin smiled and greeted him enthusiastically, looking around and responding to similar greetings. It was her first social event in Crimson Hills since she got back, and she didn't want to tell anyone why she was back; it was easier to stay away from them. Jack's patio had a gorgeous view of the surrounding countryside. The view was good even at night, with a few clusters of lights indicating the townships in the distance.

The song currently playing was "Memories" by Maroon 5, and Erin was bobbing her head side to side. "Now, how did Jack know that I liked this song?"

Garwin chuckled. "He loves this song. Maybe you can sing it at karaoke. He has the machine set up and ready to go."

Erin smiled. "I only do my singing in the shower."

She looked around; there were several familiar faces. All the people from Garwin's friend group in high school were there.

They had been two grades higher than her, and she remembered how envious she was of them then. She used to fantasize about being included in their little crew back in the day.

It was so surreal to see them now as adults.

She and Mercedes had called them the Great House crew: Derrick, Cindy, Dacy, Lee, Camille, Leighton, and Nicky. They used to hang out at the great house together. And now, here they all were. It was so comforting to see that some things remained the same.

Garwin intertwined her hand in his and walked over to the group. "Guys, here she is, my girlfriend Erin."

"Congrats! Finally, Garwin has a girlfriend!"

Erin looked at Garwin, realizing he had been serious when he said he had never been in a relationship.

A million and one hugs later, after welcoming her back to Crimson Hills, Erin found that she was enjoying herself—the music, the conversations, the food. Jill from Wimples Bakery catered for the party, and Cambria baked the cake. It was a scrumptious triple-layer chocolate, strawberry, and pistachio cake decorated like a work of art.

"I can't believe how good this tastes," Erin declared.

"Coming from Erin McMillan, chef to the stars, that's high praise," Cambria laughed. "Thank you."

Camille drifted closer to her. "Hey Erin, there is a guy going around the neighborhood asking about you."

"I heard," Erin said.

"You are not in danger, are you?" Camille asked.

"Nope," Erin shook her head. "I don't think so. I came back here to avoid someone. Unfortunately, it seems as if he found me. I'll deal with it."

Camille nodded. "I'd told the guy that we don't gossip with strangers."

"We all told him that," Cindy said, coming over. "But we do gossip among ourselves, and we've been wondering why you have been avoiding us."

"But we concluded that you will tell us whenever you are ready," Jill piped in. "So, no pressure to share."

"And we will defend you at the drop of a hat," Lee said. "You know I have my black belt in karate."

"And though I don't have a black belt, I have your back," Garwin said, squeezing her fingers.

"Thank you guys and Garwin," Erin said. "I appreciate you looking out for me."

"It's karaoke time!" Cambria clapped her hands. "Garwin usually goes first. I wonder which song he will choose tonight."

"Well, Erin is here, and I am determined to try out the

whole romance thing. So I am going to sing a song dedicated to her."

They chuckled.

"Let me see what you have in the queue," Garwin got up and searched around.

"This is exciting," Camille said, elbowing Erin. "I have never seen Garwin in love before."

Erin looked at Camille, shocked. "You think he is in love with me?"

"So you two haven't done the grand declarations yet?" Camille smiled. "Aw, I love this, and yes, Garwin is in love with you. It's as clear as day. I am just waiting for him to choose some soppy love song to confirm it."

Erin leaned forward eagerly. She wanted to hear what he would come up with.

"You know I have never heard Garwin sing before," Erin said. "Is he any good?"

"Very good," Cambria sat down near her. "Let's go, Garwin! Woo hoo!"

"Okay," Garwin started the machine. "This song is dedicated to Erin, 'You Got It' by Roy Orbison. "Every time I look into your loving eyes, I see a love that money just can't buy; one look from you, I drift away; I pray that you are here to stay…

Garwin sounded good. Erin batted away tears, especially when he did the chorus. Anything you want (you got it), Anything you need (you got it), Anything at all…

As Garwin continued to sing, his gaze remained fixed on Erin. The couples around got up and started dancing. Even Erin couldn't help herself; she started rocking, too. She was moved by the raw emotion in Garwin's performance. She felt a warmth in her heart, realizing the depth of his feelings for her. It felt like a declaration of love, and she felt every word.

Their friends were silent, captivated by the powerful moment unfolding before them. They were probably taken aback by the intensity of Garwin's rendition. It was the longer version of the song, and he even did the music riff at the end of the song.

The last note lingered in the air, and the room erupted into applause. Still looking at Erin, Garwin couldn't hide the love and vulnerability in his eyes. She felt the same, Erin realized. This was a turning point for them; this was serious territory. She wiped away a tear and embraced him.

"I think I want this song played at my wedding. Maybe the first dance."

She didn't know why she said that out loud; she didn't want Garwin to be scared away, but he just smiled.

"You got it," he whispered.

Chapter Thirteen

Garwin couldn't stop smiling. He was twenty-eight years old, and for the first time in his life, he was experiencing what people called love. Well, if it wasn't love, it certainly was a fair approximation of it; his feelings were running parallel to the song he sang at the karaoke. He really felt like he would do anything for Erin.

He sat down on the football stand with a big grin on his face even though his side, the Crimson Hill Tigers, was taking a battering on the field. It was a good thing it was a friendly match and didn't count in their group rankings, but even the parents grumbling behind him that it was his fault why the boys were taking a battering didn't shift him.

He was in a happy space. He and Erin were spending all their time together; they spent all day at the restaurant, hung out at night, and he was taking perpetual cold showers to keep his libido in check.

It was his first non-sexual, emotionally based relationship.

It was special. She was special. He wanted to feel this way forever. If he could bottle this euphoria or freeze it in time, he would.

His phone pinged; he expected it to be Erin, but it was Garnet. His sister usually texted him randomly during the day when she was excited about something. "On shore leave for two weeks," the text read.

"Are you coming to Crimson Hills?" Garwin texted.

"Yes, I want to see your pretty face," Garnet texted back, "and berate Gersham and Patti for getting married without me being there."

Garwin sent her a grinning emoji and then put away his phone.

"Your team is losing, and you are smiling," a big guy with bulging biceps sat beside him.

Garwin glanced at him and frowned. "You win some, and you lose some. Are you a parent?"

"Nope, the name is Hal Portman, detective. I work for Rafi Chan."

"Oh," Garwin glanced at him, "so no subterfuge then to get me to talk like you used on Serena?"

"No," Hal said, "a long time ago, I used to work for your grandfather. I knew your mother well; I have a soft spot for her offspring. And that's why I feel as if I should warn you about Erin," Hal said, "I know you are seeing her now, but she is not exactly single. She is still engaged to Rafi Chan."

"No, she is not," Garwin said.

"She still has his ring, though," Hal sighed. "In Rafi's estimation, that means she is engaged to him. He would like you to back off so he can pick up where he left off with his fiancé without any problems. He is a forgiving man, but he has his limits."

"What on earth?" Garwin frowned. "Are you sane?"

"Very," Hal said. "Rafi Chan is not a guy to mess with. Leave his girl alone, and there will be no trouble. Continue to see her, and there will be trouble. I can guarantee you that."

Hal got up, nodded to him, and left. Garwin's first instinct was to call Erin and tell her what he had heard, but his side scored a goal out of nowhere, and he jumped up in shock. He would talk to Erin later in the evening about the ridiculous threats he had just received.

****

Erin got in a little after six. She had been waiting for Garwin to show up at the restaurant after his football game, but he didn't. Gersham oversaw closing up, so she left the restaurant early. It gave her a chance to have a long overdue talk with her parents in private and update them on what was going on in her life.

"Why don't you come to Cayman?" Her mother was asking. "I don't see why you thought it was best to go and hide out with your grandmother, and then you left her to go and live at Miss Enid's place. Your situation sounds aimless."

"I came to Crimson Hills because this is the last place Rafi would have looked," Erin said. "I am waiting for him to marry someone, and then I can breathe a sigh of relief."

"I can't believe he wanted you to kill his father," her father said, concern in his voice. "They sound like a dangerous family, and isn't Garwin Silver, a part of this family? Why are you going out with him?"

"The Silvers and the Chans are not close," Erin said. "Remember the story of Garwin's mother escaping them and coming to Crimson Hills? He doesn't have anything to do with them, really."

"But he looks like Rafi Chan," her mother said. "I don't like this, Erin."

"He can't help it that they have a family resemblance. They are not the same person," Erin sighed. "Besides, I love Garwin."

"But of course, you think you love him," her mother said. "You have had a thing for that boy since you were a preteen."

"Is that why you went to Crimson Hills?" her father asked. "To pursue a relationship with the boy you were obsessed with when you were a young girl?"

"No," Erin sighed. "I genuinely thought this was a good place to hide, and I have been right so far. Besides, I was keeping Garwin at arm's length. I did a good job, too, but I couldn't anymore. He is the sweetest, most considerate…"

The gate buzzer went off. She expected it to be Garwin. He had probably gone home, showered, and was ready to hang with her for the evening. They had gotten embroiled with a television series on Netflix.

"I think Garwin is at the gate. Talk to you guys later."

"Wait," her mother said, concerned, "Erin, you sound like a breathless teenager who doesn't know what she is doing. Are you trying to relive your high school years?"

"No, Mom," Erin giggled. "I am trying to live my adult years with an emphasis on the word live."

"Be careful," her father said.

The buzzer sounded again.

"Thanks, Dad, I have to go. I love you guys."

She hurried to the intercom.

"Hey," she said, a smile in her voice.

"Erin, it's Rafi. Let me in; we need to talk."

Erin jumped back from the intercom like it had burned her. She was not letting this man into the house alone with her.

She didn't trust him—anyone who was willing to kill their father and use her to do it was not someone she wanted near her at all.

"No. I'm coming out," she said. She threw a wrap over her tracksuit. She didn't care how her face looked and stubbornly did not check in the mirror. She didn't want Rafi to find her attractive in any way. She walked down the winding driveway and stood about three feet from the gate. She had turned on all the lights.

He was there, dressed in black, in a turtleneck muscle shirt and black jeans, looking like a modern-day Indian prince. Seeing him in all his splendor made her realize how much like Garwin he looked. And why, for a moment, she had been captivated by him.

"So, you aren't going to let me in," Rafi smiled. "Erin, I'm harmless."

"No, you're not," Erin said.

"I would never hurt you," Rafi said. "Besides, this is no way to treat the man you will marry."

"What kind of drugs are you taking?" Erin asked seriously. "You sound delusional."

"You still have my engagement ring," Rafi said. "I just assumed that you left me because of the video. I gave you time to forgive me. Six months was enough. Here I am. You did expect me to follow you, didn't you?"

"No," Erin gasped. "I put your ring in the letter I left with Heather, and I made it clear in the letter that I am no longer interested in you.

"Nice excuse," Rafi said, "but I only got the letter, no ring. And that ring is a multi-million-dollar ring; it's a family heirloom. It is one of three rings gifted to my family by the Maharaja of Punjab long ago. My father will kill me if I don't get it back."

"You people have a serious murderous streak; your father will kill you; you tried to kill him. Rahul Chan would have killed Anya if she hadn't run away; don't you guys value life?

"Can we not discuss this in public?" Rafi said.

"Our nearest neighbor is Crimson Hill Great House, that's two miles up the road." Erin snorted.

"There are two empty lots to the left of us. This is the opposite of public."

Then she regretted telling him that. He used the word kill loosely; maybe he found their isolation perfect for his purposes.

"I expect Garwin to come by any minute now," Erin stepped back from the gate.

Rafi moved closer to the gate. "I came here to apologize to you, Erin, believe it or not. I didn't want us to start off on a bad note. My father saw the same video you saw. He forgave me for it. We are good now," Rafi said. "As you know, I inadvertently cured him. His cancer is in remission.

"He agreed that I can marry anyone I want. And I was thinking, since you already have my ring, and you have had time to cool off, that we could make a go of this."

"No, oh no," Erin said. "No offense, but I don't want to marry a man with a longstanding sexual relationship with his best friend, who is male. I know some women wouldn't mind, but I am not one of them. I am not freaky like that.

"That situation has trouble written all over it. Besides, I do not have your ring. I put it on that one time when you proposed, and then four days later, I gave it back when I saw that video. It was pretty. Nice present from the maha, whatever."

"Maharaja means king," Rafi said. "My family is related

to royalty. My ancestor was quite close to one of the kings from way back. The rings are passed down from generation to generation; the blue diamond is a first-son ring. My father gave it to me because I was about to marry someone. I managed to pay her off, and I still had the ring when I met you."

Erin took a step back. "Ah, it's all making sense to me now. Thank you for the history lesson. It is fascinating stuff. Goodnight."

"Erin," Rafi sighed, "this is serious. My father has forgiven me for trying to kill him and paying off the woman he arranged for me to marry. He will not forgive me for losing the ring. It has a family history, hundreds of years of history.

"It's a tradition to give your intended the ring upon proposal and then replace it with a platinum band after the marriage. The ring always stays with the firstborn son. It is said to have been blessed by Ganesha, the lord of success, knowledge, and wealth.

"It has not left our family till now. It is our secret weapon, our family talisman of sorts."

Erin swallowed. "Oh. But I honestly don't have it."

Rafi looked really crestfallen at that. "My solution would be marriage. We have to go through with it."

"No!" Erin said. "No!"

"My father believes you have the ring. He gave me six weeks to retrieve it. We have to at least pretend as if we are engaged, which would mean you would have a legitimate reason to have it in your possession."

"I am sorry, I can't do that," Erin said, "and I don't have that ring."

"Well, you have to find it," Rafi said. "For both our sakes. If you can find the ring and give it to me, then we can go our separate ways. But if you keep the ring, both you and I are toast. My father will see to it, and neither of us will see it coming." He stepped back. "As for that video, it can't get out. Hal said you lost your phone with the video on it."

Erin nodded, feeling paralyzed by fear. Why had she gotten mixed up with Rafi Chan with his talisman ring and his incriminating videos?

"Believe it or not, the video is the least of our worries right now," Rafi said.

A car light was coming toward them, and Rafi moved toward his car. "We will talk some more."

He drove off, leaving Erin in the driveway, her head spinning. She was an ordinary chef; she hadn't asked for all this.

Garwin drove up. Erin used the gate opener and let him in.

"Hey," he stopped. "You look like you just got bad news."

"I did," Erin walked with him as he slowly drove up the driveway.

Erin opened the front door with trembling fingers. "Rafi came to see me."

"Oh, so that was him driving down the hill. I wondered whose Rolls Royce that was. It is unusual to see that kind of vehicle on these hills," Garwin said. "I expected he would show up after his private investigator warned me off today. He said you and Rafi are still engaged because you have the Chan diamond."

"That's the same thing that Rafi said," Erin laughed dryly. "Can you imagine that I have been hiding all this time, waiting for Rafi to marry someone else, only to find out that he thinks we are still engaged!"

"Why would he think that?" Garwin frowned.

"Because the Chan diamond he gave me when he proposed is not just a run-of-the-mill engagement ring. Apparently, it was a family heirloom blessed by one of the Hindu Gods, Lord Ganesh, gifted by royalty, and passed down through several generations."

"In other words, quite important," Garwin nodded.

"Oh yes," Erin said. "And I just put it in the letter I left for him before I fled St. Lucia, and he said he didn't get it."

"Maybe he's lying," Garwin said.

"No, he wasn't," Erin ran her fingers through her hair in frustration. "He looked really scared when I said I didn't have it. That look was real. It scared me too."

Garwin snorted.

"I believe him," Erin said. "He knows his father better than we do. His solution is that we should pretend to still be engaged, and that would extend our chances to live."

"Hell no," Garwin said.

"If I don't marry him, his father will kill us both," Erin said.

"Ridiculous," Garwin said.

"Not ridiculous. It's a family heirloom given to them by some ruling king in India's distant past. The ring was always given to the first son. Apparently, the Chan family was related to royalty."

"Is that so?" Garwin grinned. "I didn't even know India had a royal family."

"They did for hundreds of years. They became a republic in the seventies," Erin said.

"It kind of explains the Chan fixation on marrying people from specific families in India," Garwin mused. "I guess they are trying to maintain that connection. It makes sense now in a weird kind of way."

"I guess," Erin sighed.

"So let me get this straight," Garwin leaned forward. "You gave the secretary the letter with the ring in it?"

"Yes, Jodi's secretary, Heather. I gave her the letter. She said she would give it to Rafi."

"But he got the letter with no ring," Garwin shook his head. "She took that ring. What did it look like?"

"It was a big square blue diamond, like the color of the sky. I remember when Rafi gave it to me; I was shocked at how pretty it was. I had never seen anything like it before. Unsurprisingly, I am not big on jewelry; I hardly wear any because of the job. I was already feeling nervous because of how expensive it was. To be frank, it was a relief to get it out of my custody."

"Heather probably saw it and saw dollar signs," Garwin said.

Erin nodded. "She was very specific about putting the ring in the letter, too, and I naively did it all because I didn't want to face Rafi with what I knew."

"Call her and tell her that Rafi is looking for it and if she could please give it to him because you don't want any trouble," Garwin said.

Erin inhaled. "If only it were that simple."

"At least try," Garwin said. "You never know what the outcome could be. Do you want to use my phone?"

"No," Erin started pacing. "I am good. I have unlimited international minutes; I always call my parents."

Garwin sat back and watched her as she dialed Heather's number and then hung up.

"She's not answering," Erin said in despair.

"Because she probably recognizes your number. Give it a couple of minutes and call from my phone," Garwin said.

"What if she lost it?" Erin asked. "What if she didn't steal it? What if it fell out of the envelope in the bushes beside the house, and is lying in wait until someone finds it."

Garwin chuckled, "You sound like me when I was a child.

I call it magical thinking. I didn't want to face reality. I would fantasize that my dad would come home sober and smiling and declare to us that he wasn't going to drink anymore. He would apologize, and we would live happily ever after. None of my fantasy scenarios ever happened. So, as an adult, I explore all the realistic scenarios that can happen and then face them head-on before I resort to magical thinking."

"Okay, no magical thinking," Erin nodded. "So, in scenario one, Heather stole and sold the ring."

Garwin nodded. "Or scenario two, Heather stole the ring and still has it. Fencing an expensive heirloom piece like that isn't that easy."

"I agree," Erin inhaled. "I am going to call Jody Rogan, tell her what happened, and appeal to her to speak to Heather."

Garwin nodded.

Erin dialed Jody's number.

Jody answered pleasantly, quite pleased to hear from her. After telling her what happened, Jody was aghast.

"Heather doesn't work with me anymore, Erin. I realized that she was stealing from me. I decided against prosecuting her, but hearing from you now, I regret that decision."

"Do you have any idea where she is?" Erin asked, her heart racing.

"Not a clue," Jody said. "She lived here on the island but had ties in the US."

"Thanks, Jody." Erin hung up and looked across at Garwin. "Heather is gone. The ring is gone, and I," she swallowed, "I'll have to marry Rafi Chan."

Chapter Fourteen

Garwin drove home; it was a little after twelve, and he would soon get up to open the store. But he knew he wouldn't be getting much sleep tonight. He couldn't allow Erin to marry Rafi just because she couldn't find a ring. He would have to marry her first, and then Rafi and Samir would have to deal with him.

He tossed and turned and thought about it all night into the wee hours of the morning. He knew what he had to do. It was so simple. The thing is, he could imagine himself with Erin for the rest of his life. But he would pitch it to her as a temporary solution to her problems. It was the perfect solution for their situation right now, for her situation.

He got up and had an ice cold shower to wake himself up. Gersham and Patti were already in the driveway when he went outside.

"You two are up early," he said.

"I am driving to Kingston," Patti said. "I have to sort out

my passport. I didn't realize it expires in a few days. Garnet said she'd hitch a ride with me on the way back."

Garwin nodded, "Wait before you go," he said before Patti entered her vehicle. "What do you think of me marrying Erin?"

"Say what now?" Patti frowned. Gersham looked at him in shock.

"You heard me," Garwin said. Patti grinned. "Oh, this is a prank. Play along, Gersham."

"No, I'm serious," Garwin said. "I stayed up all night thinking about it. Here's the scenario. Rafi asked Patti to marry him because if she doesn't, Samir Chan will kill them both."

"But why?" Patti and Gersham asked at the same time.

Rafi proposed to her and gave her a family heirloom ring. When she left St. Lucia, she put the ring in a letter and gave it to her boss's secretary to give to Rafi. Now the ring can't be found. Samir is mad as hell about that. Rafi's solution is for them to get married anyway to throw his father off their scent.

"Why did she turn down Rafi in the first place?" Patti frowned, "isn't he Jamaica's most eligible bachelor?"

"She saw a video of him planning to use her to kill his father by poisoning his food."

"Oh," Patti grimaced. "I did tell her I didn't want to hear about that. That would make for a juicy article."

"So he was the one who was poisoning Samir," Gersham shook his head, "their family is crazy."

"The poisoning helped Samir," Garwin said, "and apparently, he is not holding it against Rafi, so he can marry anybody he wants now."

"Oh boy," Gersham finally said.

"So Erin wrote him a letter, returned the ring with the

letter, and left it with the co-worker. And now, Rafi is here, wants the video deleted, and wants back the ring. If she doesn't give him back the ring, then she will have to marry him, or else his murderous father will take it on."

"Okay, that's a lot to unpack," Gersham said.

"Yeah, there's even more," Garwin said. "The phone is lost. Patti can't find it. And the co-worker who was given the letter and the ring is no longer working at the place. She vanished into thin air. With the ring!"

"Oh wow," Patti said.

I was thinking a perfect solution would be for her to marry me. Rafi can't marry her when she's married to me. That's not allowed in this country. And then, while we're married, we try to find that ring."

"Ah, makes perfect sense," Patti said. "Especially since you love her anyway."

"I do love her, but marriage is a step I hadn't even considered until now." Garwin frowned. "I'm helping out a friend."

Gersham chuckled. "If any other friend was in this predicament, would you be helping them out with marriage?"

Garwin frowned. "Nope."

"So, would this be a real marriage?" Patti asked.

"Well, I haven't thought past the ceremony part," Garwin said. And getting her out of this obligation that Rafi thinks she should have and marry him."

"I see," Patti nodded, "well, I'm all for it," Patti said.

"I don't know," Gersham said. "It sounds logical, but isn't there another solution? Marrying her will not automatically solve the problem of her finding the ring. Her life will still be in danger."

"And I'll protect her." Garwin said, "If Samir Chan wants to kill her over a ring that she has, well, he is even more of a lunatic than I thought."

"Maybe he is a lunatic; I don't like the idea of us butting heads with that family again; our mother ran away to escape them; she did it for a reason. They are not jokers, Garwin."

"I know, that's why I have to step in and help Erin," Garwin said. "And this seems to be the best solution."

"Well, okay," Gersham sounded unsure. "So when would this marriage take place?"

"I haven't even told Erin the plan yet," Garwin said. "But I'm assuming the sooner, the better. She can get Rafi off her case."

"Oh, man, I'm leaving just when Crimson Hill is about to get juicy," Patti said.

"But you'll be back tomorrow, babe," Gersham said. "I don't think he'll be getting married before tomorrow. He has to ask the girl first, and she has to say yes."

****

"What's your answer, Erin?" Rafi seemed to materialize from beside the wall when she exited the side gate.

"How long were you lurking out here?" Erin hissed. "You even parked your car further down the road. You are sneaky."

"I haven't been out here that long. I know you are supposed to be at the restaurant by six. I can give you a lift if you want."

Erin wanted badly to tell him she wasn't interested, but she had woken up late because she was overthinking things for most of the night, and she hadn't yet gone to her grandmother's place for the bicycle.

In the wee hours of the morning, she had come up with a solution; she would bolt again. She had a granduncle, her grandmother's brother, who lived in a little village in the Blue Mountains. Rafi wouldn't be able to find her there, but the ring would still be missing, and she couldn't hide forever. They would think she stole it and was hiding.

"I can't marry you," Erin said, "that's a crazy solution. Surely your father won't kill us over a ring."

Rafi laughed dryly. "I don't want to find out what he would do."

"I called Heather last night, but she didn't answer, so I called Jody. Jody said Heather left their employ a few months ago because of theft. I think we can both assume what happened to the ring."

"She still lives in St. Lucia, right?" Rafi asked.

"She used to," Erin said. "I don't know where she is now. You have the resources to track her down. Find her. The quicker you do, the better we will all be."

"I'll make some calls," Rafi said.

"Yes, please. I want all of this cleared up and put behind me."

Rafi opened the passenger door, and Erin got in.

Rafi turned to her. "If you marry me, I would buy you your own restaurant. You wouldn't have to be slogging it away in the country cooking basic meals."

"I like it here," Erin said, "and there is no way I'd marry you after seeing you in bed with Rich Rogan plotting to kill your father. I am not that hard up for riches."

"We could make it a business marriage," Rafi said. "We'd need to have children, though. At least two to satisfy my obligations to the Chan line."

"No, thank you," Erin said. "After saying yes to your proposal before, I was filled with doubts. I want to marry for love, and the thing is, I didn't love you even then. I was a bit star-struck and very flattered that the guy who resembled my teenage crush was willing to give me some attention and even marry me. I don't think I genuinely liked you. I was caught up in the moment."

"Woah," Rafi started the car. "Is this bash my ego day?"

"Sorry," Erin shrugged. "Sometimes, some hard truths are required. We were both, in a way, using each other. You wanted a chef to kill your father, and I wanted a rich, handsome guy to sweep me off my feet to live the fantasy. Without seeing that video, I wonder if the fantasy would have come crashing down around me and if I would have actually gone through with it."

"I think I would have made a really good husband," Rafi said.

"To Rich," Erin said, "not to me."

"Speaking of Rich," Rafi didn't bother to deny her rebuttal, "are you sure you aren't just keeping that video to blackmail me in the future?"

"Very sure," Erin said. "I had it on my phone, thinking that if you ever came looking for me and trying to convince me to marry you, I would show it to you as leverage for you to leave me alone. I thought you were a dangerous criminal then, and I still think so now."

"I am mostly harmless," Rafi drove up to the restaurant. "I never committed a crime before attempting to hasten my father to death's door. But the thing is, I can't say the same for my dad. And Erin, know this: you don't want to be in my father's crosshairs, so like me or not, you'll have to marry me if we can't find that ring and bluff our way out of this. My father made a big concession: I could marry whoever I wanted. Surely we can come to some agreement where you stay married to me until he dies."

"No," Erin said, "hell no. We have to find Heather and that ring."

Rafi clenched his jaw. "Okay. We'll do it your way for now, but we don't have much time. You have two weeks to think about this, Erin. I have to go to St. Lucia to sort out some business; maybe there I will find Heather and get back the ring. If not, we are both in serious trouble."

"Fine," Erin said.

Chapter Fifteen

"I've been thinking about my situation all day," Erin said to Garwin. The restaurant was closed; they were in the courtyard alone. Only the sound of the reggae classics could be heard in the background.

This was the first chance they had gotten to talk privately. They had two events to cater to and a busier-than-usual day with back-to-back customers from the great house tour. They had to double up the food output, which meant all three of the chefs were in the kitchen. Gersham had just left, vowing to hire another chef, which was good because Erin was seriously thinking of making a run for it, and she didn't want to leave them in the lurch.

"I've been thinking about your situation too," Garwin said. "The more I think about it, the more I think you should…"

"Run away again?" Erin said. "I spoke to Rafi this morning; he said he would find Heather. I will come out of hiding when he finds her and retrieves his ring."

"No," Garwin frowned. "You are my girlfriend now,

remember? I don't want you to leave me. What if he never finds her or his ring? You can't run forever."

"True," Erin sighed. "So true. I am sick and tired of hiding. But I can't marry Rafi. Not even as a business marriage. I would rather be at the mercy of Samir Chan."

"Well, you could marry me," Garwin said. "Rafi can't insist on marriage if you are already married. It's the perfect solution."

Erin stared at Garwin, transfixed for the longest time. She wasn't sure she had heard right, but her heart had picked up speed, beating like a drum on hyper speed.

"Think about it," Garwin moved closer. "Getting married will be perfect for us. We are already friends; we work together, have the same interests, and love the same shows and music. The way we are attracted to each other, I am sure we will be dynamite in bed together."

Erin nodded. "But marriage is a bit drastic, don't you think?"

"But so is your other proposal," Garwin said. "Running away is drastic. Rafi Chan would only find you again, and then what? You would be forced to marry a man who repulses you through no fault of your own, you lost his expensive engagement ring, and his murderous father will kill you. I mean, you can't make up this kind of thing."

"I know," Erin nodded. "I feel like I have been living like a character in a soap opera."

Garwin grinned.

"I can't believe you would propose marriage," Erin said. "I am surprised, shocked even. Would this be a serious marriage?"

"I didn't know they had comical ones," Garwin said.

"You know what I mean," Erin said. "Is this a forever kind of thing? Or is this just about helping me out?"

"What do you want?" Garwin asked.

"I want it to be real," Erin said. "I want to get married because of normal reasons, you know. Reasons like you love me and can't live without me. I don't want to get married because someone wants me to kill their father or because you don't want that same father to kill me. The first reason is crazy. The second reason is not much better."

Garwin intertwined their fingers together. "Erin, I don't want to lose you and can't afford to run away to the hills with you. I have a business to run."

Erin smiled. "I know that."

"So I say, we give this marriage thing a try. We could make it temporary long enough to throw off Rafi and his father. Once they find their ring, we can return to our normal life."

Erin shook her head. "I am giving that a hard pass, sorry."

"I like you a lot. I have never felt this way about anybody before. I don't know if it's love. I do know I don't want you to be hurt, and I do know that you bring out my protective instincts. And I feel jealous as hell to think of you marrying Rafi Chan. I don't care if it is for show. I don't want you tied to that kooky family."

Erin laughed. "Garwin, you do realize that you are a part of that family."

"Yes, but the Silver side of me balances out the madness."

Erin chuckled. "I am appreciative of your honesty, Garwin. I really am…"

"Hear that?" Garwin put a finger over her lips. It was Bob Marley's song, 'Is This Love.'

I wanna love you, and treat you right, I wanna love you every day and every night… Is this love, is this love that I am feeling…"

He moved closer to her. "I couldn't have chosen a more appropriate song for the moment." He started singing along with Bob Marley, "I am willing and able, so I'll throw all the cards on the table..."

Erin started singing along with him. They rocked and sang together, diffusing what was, until then, a serious moment.

Erin started laughing when the song ended. "I am convinced there will never be a dull moment between us."

Garwin grinned. "We'll share the shelter of my single bed."

"Is your bed really single?" Erin asked.

"Nope." Garwin shook his head. "King size."

Erin grinned.

"How about this?" Garwin cupped her cheek. "We'll work on the question, 'Is this love that we are feeling,' while we live as man and wife, and we'll embrace the marriage wholeheartedly and then reassess things on our first anniversary. We could check the temperature of our union and see if we want to stay together."

"That doesn't sound like a bad idea," Erin nodded. "A yearly assessment to see the state of our union."

Garwin nodded, pressing his forehead on hers. "I am looking forward to you being in my king-sized bed." He placed his lips on hers and kissed her briefly.

"There is more where that came from," he pulled away.

"My friends will be shocked; I introduced you as my girlfriend a few days ago."

"My parents are going to want to come to the wedding," Erin said, "and they will want to know what the rush is about. What will I tell them?"

"That love can't wait," Garwin chuckled.

"When and where would we get married?" Erin asked. "Can we pull off a wedding in two weeks?"

"Of course, sure," Garwin nodded. "Why two weeks, though?"

"Rafi is coming back by then. He has gone to St. Lucia."

"I see, or we could elope," Garwin said. "Just us at a courthouse, with two witnesses, and then tell everybody after."

"Good," Erin sighed in relief.

"Should we get a ring?" Garwin asked.

"No," Erin said, "It's not as if I can wear it in the kitchen. Maybe we can get two plain bands for the ceremony. When Rafi gave me the big old diamond, I only put it on that one time."

"This proposal is far different than the one with him, isn't it?" Garwin asked, a hint of jealousy in his voice.

"Oh, so different," Erin grinned. "It was over the top and romantic and totally fake. He wanted me to commit murder, remember?"

Garwin grinned. "I tend to forget. I got jealous for a while."

Erin moved closer to Garwin and rested her head on his shoulder. "I can't believe we are doing this."

"Me neither," Garwin said. "Maybe we should go through with it before it sinks in."

"Yes," Erin nodded and then yawned. "I am so sleepy."

"Me too," Garwin said. "I didn't get a wink of sleep last night; I stayed up thinking about a solution to this mess you got yourself in, Chef McMillan."

Erin chuckled. "Thank you for thinking about me, Chef Silver."

****

Garwin dropped Erin home and didn't bother to go inside; they both needed to mull over their decision. He wondered why he wasn't doubtful or scared; he had quickly adopted the idea.

When he drove up, the light was on in the center part of the house; he knew his father wasn't due back for weeks. He parked on his side and stepped over to his father's side. Gersham and Larry had a building plan on the dining table between them. They were looking over the extension plans.

"Oh," Garwin said, "I quite forgot the text from earlier today."

"I figured," Gersham said, "I know you have a lot on your plate."

"Quite a bit," Garwin said, "but that shouldn't have prevented me from remembering this. You wanted me to be in charge of the project."

"But Larry said he can start tomorrow," Gersham said, "so I'll be around for this."

"I am glad you'll be around to oversee this," Garwin said, "What's up, Larry?"

"Nothing much," Larry said, "are we still on for Sunday?"

"What's happening on Sunday again?" Garwin asked.

"Charity football match against Cascade Hills," Larry frowned. "Don't let me down, man; you are our star striker. We owe it to the Crismon Hills basic school community to win."

"Of course," Garwin nodded.

"I have never seen the man like this," Larry turned to Gersham, "he is high on Erin; I bet she is the reason for the memory lapses."

Garwin nodded. "She kinda is."

"I am happy for you," Larry said, "congrats, man."

After Larry left, Gersham looked at him skeptically, "So you asked her?"

"I did," Garwin nodded, "and she said yes. Her solution was to run away again; I made her see the futility of that. We are thinking of doing a courthouse wedding and then telling everybody after."

Gersham frowned. "And you are sure you want to do this?"

"Never been surer," Garwin said. "And I want you to be one of my witnesses."

"I'll be there," Gersham said. "Regardless of whether I approve of the haste of this or not. When's the date?"

"We haven't decided yet," Garwin said, "it's definitely not Sunday, though. I have that match."

Chapter Sixteen

"**T**his rush to get married because you want to foil somebody's plan to rush you into marriage is not a good reason to get married." Mercedes looked at both Erin and Garwin sternly. "However, I am not here to talk you out of marriage; I am here to make sure that you both know what you are getting into."

Erin groaned. "I thought we were going to tell everyone after we did it. How did Mercedes know?"

"I told Gersham," Garwin said. "I wanted him to be a witness."

"And he told Patti, and Patti told me," Mercedes smiled. "So, I took it upon myself to get over here after closing hours to see if we can do some speed premarital counseling. This is an unconventional situation, so it has to be unconventional therapy."

"You've been married for five minutes," Garwin snorted. "What are you going to tell us about marriage?"

Mercedes smiled. "Please be respectful, Mr. Silver. You are not paying me for this, and may I remind you that I am a fully qualified psychotherapist."

Erin hid a grin. "Are you going to be calling me Miss McMillan?"

"I am not sure yet," Mercedes leaned back in her seat. "It depends on your attitude."

They were in the seating area of the restaurant. Music played in the background. Today was supposed to be gospel day, and Mira, who usually chose gospel music, was currently in love with soca afrobeats.

It put Erin in good spirits. She was bobbing her head to Dajourney, Never Fail.

"Would you like a drink? Something to eat?" Erin asked. "I can make grilled cheese sandwiches and soup. We ran out of food at dinner, and still, we have zero leftovers today."

"Okay, now we are talking," Mercedes grinned. "Grilled cheese sandwiches and soup sounds perfect."

"I'll get it," Garwin got up. "Do you want anything, Erin?"

"No, I am fine," Erin smiled. "I had a massive cobb salad for lunch."

"That's why you stay so fit," Mercedes said. "I wondered how you maintained your figure around all this food."

"I am on my feet a lot, and I eat a fair amount of salads," Erin said. "And since I've been here, I have been cycling up and down the hill daily. My calves are rock hard. I am thinking of getting myself a vehicle, though. It's high time. Cycling is not fun in the rain."

"That's a coincidence," Mercedes said, "because I am selling mine. My dad bought me a car as a wedding present. It doesn't make much sense that Charles and I keep three vehicles. I haven't decided on a price though; you will be the first to know when I do."

Garwin brought the soup.

"It smells so good," Mercedes inhaled it. "Thank you. I am blessed to have chefs as friends. While I am eating, I would like you to peruse this one-page premarital questionnaire."

She rummaged in her briefcase and handed them both separate papers and pens.

Erin smiled. "You haven't changed much from high school; you are still organized and efficient."

"And bossy," Garwin grumbled. "And nosy."

Mercedes chuckled. "I will take all of your complaints as compliments."

Erin glanced through the questionnaire. There were questions covering various aspects of their relationship, values, and future plans. She looked up at Mercedes with a quizzical expression.

"So, are we supposed to fill this out right now?" Erin asked, taking a sip of her water.

Mercedes nodded. "Yes, right now. I need to understand your perspectives and expectations before we dive into any counseling. This will help us address potential areas of concern and ensure a smoother transition into married life."

Garwin sighed but started filling out the questionnaire. "Where are we going to live?" Erin looked over at Garwin and grinned. "At your place, of course."

"Good," Garwin nodded, "you have never been to my place. I am going to have to give you a tour."

Mercedes silently watched the two of them as they went through the questions. She finished her meal and sat back.

"Done," Erin said first.

"Almost done," Garwin looked up. He finished writing with a flourish and handed the questionnaire to Mercedes. She began reviewing the responses.

"Good, good," she murmured, nodding as she compared

the responses. "You both seem to have a solid foundation and are remarkably in tune with each other about your general likes and dislikes. Let's discuss some points you've raised here: finances, religion, and communication styles."

For the next hour, they delved into various aspects of their relationship, addressing concerns, expectations, and hopes for the future.

Erin realized in the middle of speaking at one point that she was talking to her childhood friend, and she was really good at her job. She glanced at Garwin, too, and she knew the moment it hit him that this meeting with Mercedes may not have been planned, but it was necessary. Despite the rushed circumstances, they were fortunate to have her guidance.

"Okay," Mercedes said when the little alarm clock in her bag went off. "My hour is up. But we have covered the groundwork for a strong marriage: mutual respect, understanding, compromise, and speaking each other's love language. Of course, all of this is just lip service, and the proof of the pudding is in the eating, as the saying goes."

She started packing up her things.

"Wait a minute, you had us on actual time."

"Of course," Mercedes snickered. "And you don't want to know how much I charge per hour." She handed them back the questionnaire. "Go home, look it over, discuss the finer details together, but I conclude that you are both compatible. There are no glaring red flags that I can see here. You have the basic framework for a long-lasting marriage; the rest is up to you.

"That is my opinion as your counselor; as your friend, I wouldn't mind celebrating with you both, which would mean a well-planned wedding that is not quite as rushed. You both have a significant family network, not to mention friends who are family. Imagine their disappointment if they don't celebrate with you."

"That's food for thought," Erin said. "But the whole reason we are rushing is that I don't have to marry Rafi Chan; we want to preempt him."

"And if there was no Rafi Chan," Mercedes asked skeptically, "would you two be marrying each other?"

"I don't know," Erin looked at Garwin.

"It is a possibility," Garwin said, "who knows..."

Chapter Seventeen

It was late evening when Garwin got in. It had been a long day. Garnet was waiting for him in his living room, eating popcorn and watching television.

"Hey, big bro," Garnet got up and hugged him. "Tell me everything. Patti tried her best to keep me updated about the interesting turn your life has taken, but I want to hear it from the horse's mouth."

"Of course," Garwin looked her over. "You lost weight, and you grew your hair out. I haven't seen you with your hair long since you were a little girl."

"I was a part of this musical, and I had to wear this wig," Garnet laughed. "It itched like crazy, so I decided to grow out my own hair. Best decision I ever made."

"Makes sense," Garwin nodded.

"As for the weight loss, I've been doing hot yoga. I do it every day. It's addicting. I am going to miss it. Do you know if anybody does hot yoga in Kingston?"

"How would I know that?" Garwin sat down on the settee

across from her. "Isn't all yoga hot in the Kingston heat?"

"No dummy, it's a type of yoga where they turn up the temperature in the room, usually between 95 and 105 degrees Fahrenheit, to enhance the benefits. It's intense, but the heat helps with flexibility, detoxification, and weight loss." Garnet laughed. "I missed you."

"I missed you too," Garwin said. "When are you coming back home for a while?"

"Now," Garnet said, "my contract is up. I am not renewing it. I am back for good. Since Gersham blessed me with a few million dollars, I no longer have to work so hard. I can make a vanity album and spend some time with my kid. He acts as if he doesn't know me anymore. Aunt Joy had to tell him, 'Neon, that's mommy.' The kid insists on calling me Miss. He is doing it for spite, I tell you, but I am mortified. How did I become that person where my own offspring doesn't know me?"

Garwin smiled. "The point is, you are here now. He is just four; he won't remember you were gone for most of his life."

"True," Garnet frowned, "do you remember when you were four?"

"Not really," Garwin said. "My childhood up until age seven is a blur. I remember the beatings, the broken fingers, Dad coming toward me with a machete to chop my head off, Dad hovering over me with a pillow to stifle me to death, Dad…"

Garnet gasped. "Stop. I forgot how terrible your childhood was. I am so happy I don't remember any of it, really."

"You were four when mom died," Garwin said. "When Aunt Joy came to live with us, and dad went to jail. You had a normal childhood."

Garnet nodded. "I did have a normal childhood and I keep

telling myself that. Aunt Joy was the one who raised me, and she is doing the same for Neon. But I can't help but feel that maybe it's not fair to her, you know. She did her job with me; I should be in my son's life."

Garwin nodded. "And his father?"

"Out of the picture," Garnet laid back in the settee.

"I know who he is," Garwin said.

"No, you don't," Garnet said. "I will not tell a soul."

"I went to Jack Knight's birthday party."

"So?" Garnet shrugged. "His father is not Jack Knight."

"I know," Garwin chuckled. "But Neon looks a little like Jack. And then your big secret was unraveled in my head. Neon Silver is Chex Knight Hastings' son."

"Fascinating deduction, but why Chex?" Garnet asked. "It could be the other brother, Phillip."

"Nope, it's Chex. It adds up; he is a record producer, and you are a singer. I am guessing you had a thing with him that summer and then became pregnant. Jack always says Chex doesn't want children, so I will assume you didn't tell him because of that."

"Correct on all fronts," Garnet sighed. "I fell in love with a playboy producer, had his kid, and I have been running ever since."

"Why run?" Garwin asked.

"I was addicted to him; I had to break the addiction," Garnet sighed. "There was no future with Chex. Besides the fact that Chex would freak out if he found out I had his child, he has this thing where he doesn't want to perpetuate his father's genes. He is dead serious when it comes to not procreating."

"Besides that, he has daddy issues, relationship issues, fear of commitment issues, and is emotionally stunted. I left him when I found out I was pregnant and never looked back.

I didn't want to go through the indignity of being asked to have an abortion or listen to the reasons why we can't work out. I preempted him, walked away, and never looked back."

"His family would welcome Neon with open arms," Garwin said. "It dawned on me that Jack is one of my best friends, and he and I share the same nephew, but he doesn't know."

"And it will stay that way," Garnet growled.

"Okay," Garwin held up his hand. "I get the message. It's your business, and you will handle it how you see fit."

"Enough about me and my life," Garnet said. "It's time to put you in the spotlight. What's this I hear about you and marriage? Why are you marrying Erin McMillan in a rush?"

"It's not a rush," Garwin said. "I am helping her out."

"Well, well, well," Garnet giggled. "That's quite altruistic of you. I am sure the girls in your past would be crushed to know that all they needed to do was to be threatened with marriage from another man, and Garwin would come racing to the rescue."

Garwin threw a pillow at her.

"So when is the date?" Garnet asked.

"Sometime in the next two weeks," Garwin said.

"Okay," Garnet said, "I'll come down for it because you are not having a wedding without me. Not while I'm here."

"I only need two witnesses," Garwin said.

"Well, you'll be getting three," Garnet snorted.

"So no advice," Garwin said.

"Nope," Garnet said, "I trust you know what you're doing. I met this old couple on a cruise once. They've been married for 60 years. And you know what the lady said their special formula was?"

"What?" Garwin asked.

"Any marriage can work if you just give and take a

little without losing yourself, lay off the selfishness, think about the other person's needs, and voila, 60 years," Garnet grinned. "That's all there is to it, apparently. Besides, you have a good template to work with."

"What good template?" Garwin asked.

"You see all the marriages crumbling around you, cheating, abuse, you name it. Just do the opposite of what the failing marriages do and please your girl, every day and every night."

Garwin laughed. "That's not bad advice."

"Now you're making me sound wise," Garwin grinned. "And we all know that where relationships are concerned, I don't know crap."

"Welcome home, sis." Garwin grinned.

"It's good to be back, bro."

Chapter Eighteen

Erin made her way towards her grandmother's house. She didn't need to be at the restaurant until it was time for the dinner service. It felt good getting up late. She imagined that Serena would have carried the children to school by now and her grandmother would be there alone. She heard her grandmother before she reached the gate. She was sweeping off the veranda and cussing to herself.

"I want them out, gone," Miss Betty grumbled. "Why do I have to put up with this, Father God? Why me?"

Erin smiled. Serena's stay was on shaky ground.

"Gan Gan?" Erin said softly. "What are you mumbling about?"

"Erin," Miss Betty said. "Come look here in the living room."

Erin walked into the living room. There was a shopping bag overflowing with things on one of the settees. "What am I looking at?" she asked.

"Serena's wildebeest son's loot," Miss Betty said. "That

boy has been stealing and storing my things in a bag under the bed."

"Oh," Erin looked over in the bag. There was a gold purse, a jewel case, her grandmother's black and gold pearls that she wore to funerals, and two bottles of perfume with stylish gold tops. And her phone in the gold case.

"That's my phone," Erin said, grabbing it up.

"I didn't even realize your phone was in there," Miss Betty said. "Serena's going to have to move out with her kleptomaniac. Not another day."

Erin hugged the phone to her. She didn't even hear the rest of her grandmother's complaints. Now, she had to charge it, show it to Rafi, and let him delete the video for himself.

"Are you hearing me, Erin?" Miss Betty asked. "You have space at the Rafferty place? Let her move in with you."

"I can't do that, Gan Gan," Erin said. "Patti and Gersham are my friends, and they're allowing me to stay in one little room at the place. I moved out to escape Serena, not to have her move in with me.

"Can you imagine the number of things that boy would steal if he lived at Miss Enid's place? The place is a treasure trove of history."

"What's he going to do with them, though?" Miss Betty asked.

"It seems as if he took the gold things. My phone case has a gold cover."

"Ah," Miss Betty said. "What do you call it when people are attracted to gold things?"

"A gold digger?" Erin chuckled.

Miss Betty frowned. "Erin, be serious. This is probably a medical condition he should be committed to the hospital with it."

Erin laughed. "That's a creative way to have them move

out but I am leaving you alone with that. I came here to ask to borrow the bicycle. I will only be needing it for a few weeks more. Mercedes said she's selling her car and I might buy it."

"No problem, take it," Miss Betty said. "It's a good thing it doesn't have any gold on it, or else this little boy would have it under his bed."

Erin laughed. "Cut them some slack, Gan Gan. They are your family; this is a refuge."

"I'm going to have to lock my room door now," Miss Betty muttered.

Erin went for the bicycle, which was at its spot, leaning up at the side of the house. "Thanks, Gan Gan. By the way, if you hear that I'm living with Garwin Silver, please don't panic. We will be making it legal. It's just that I'm not broadcasting it."

"Okay," Miss Betty said. "So you're getting married in secret. Good for you, girl. It's nobody's business if you think about it."

"That's quite liberal of you, Gan Gan, so you aren't mad that I'm not having a large wedding or anything like that?" Erin asked.

"No," Miss Betty said. "I'm actually happy for you. I've always liked that Garwin. Besides, your grandfather and I never got married. Who am I to talk."

"What?" Erin paused.

"The man and I were perpetually engaged," Miss Betty said. "Only to find out that he had another family in St. Mary. He abandoned us here in Crimson Hills and returned to his family in St. Mary. And from then on, he has been dead to me, but everybody assumes I'm a widow."

"He is still alive?" Erin frowned. "Does mom know this?"

"Of course she does," Miss Betty said. "We pretend as if

he isn't alive, though."

"So my grandfather is still alive?" Erin asked. "Imagine that."

"Yep," Miss Betty said. "Trust me, you have not missed out on knowing him."

Erin leaned up on the bicycle and came to sit down. "Tell me more."

"There's really nothing more to tell," Miss Betty said. "I was with him for ten years, and then I found out he was a lying, cheating piece of crap. So we parted ways. He abandoned his children and me. That was eons ago."

"Okay, then," Erin said. "Why are you telling me this now?"

"I didn't want you feeling guilty about not having a wedding," Miss Betty snorted. "What's a wedding anyway?"

"True," Erin said.

"It's the marriage you need to worry about." Miss Betty continued sweeping and started humming.

****

When she went to work, the place had changed significantly. The empty lot adjoining the restaurant was being prepped for construction. "I can't believe how fast this is happening," she said when she went to the kitchen.

"Yep, Larry said he'd do it in six weeks," Gersham said. "If you and Garwin could hold off a bit, we could have our first wedding there."

"Now that would be awesome," Erin said.

"What would be awesome?" Garwin asked when he came into the kitchen.

"Gersham was saying that if we held off until the events place next door is finished, then we could get married over there," Erin said.

"Are you two getting married for real, or is this a joke?" Fred, the prep cook, asked.

"It's a secret," Garwin said. "Pretend as if you're not hearing us."

Fred laughed. "Well, if you are getting married, congratulations. I feel so bad now that I didn't shoot my shot with Erin when I could."

"I'm happy you didn't," Erin said, "because Nan would come to the restaurant and beat me up."

Nan was Fred's girlfriend, and she was very possessive of him.

Fred laughed. "Nan has changed. She's going to church and stuff. She is a Christian now; she is thinking twice before beating up people these days or cussing out people in the bus park."

Tammy looked up from her food preparation. "So the next wedding, in the new place, will be Chef Garwin and Chef Erin. I have never been to a chef-themed wedding before; I've seen it on TV on one of the food shows I watch. Will you two be cooking the food?"

"No," Gersham said, "I would do the cooking, and I'd expect Jill to do the cake."

"What's a chef themed wedding anyway?" Garwin asked. "Assuming we would have a wedding like that instead of going to a courthouse."

"It's a wedding where every element revolves around the culinary world," Tammy explained, wiping her hands on a kitchen towel. "From the invitations shaped like recipe cards to the décor resembling a sophisticated kitchen, a chef-themed wedding is a celebration of love with a dash of culinary flair."

"The menu is the focal point, featuring the couple's

favorite dishes or a selection of gourmet foods that nobody has had before. We'd have to taste test them here before we spring it on the crowd, though."

"So basically," Fred said, "it's all about food. It would be lit."

"Yes," Garwin grinned, "two chefs getting married would be a feast."

"Nobody would be coming to our wedding expecting the ordinary," Erin said, "I would make it into a culinary experience they won't forget. It would be the talk of the town."

"Nope, the talk of the country when we are done," Garwin said. "We couldn't allow Gersham to do it himself. We would have to help. Jill can work her magic with the pastries."

Gersham grinned. "Now you two have to get married. You have us all excited at the prospect of it."

****

"So, have you thought of a date yet?" Garwin asked when the restaurant was closed. They were turning off the lights and heading outside.

"No," Erin said. "Have you thought of anything?"

"Not yet," Garwin said. "But I have been thinking about doing this all day."

He closed the door and turned off the overhead lights. Then he leaned there upon the door and kissed her.

As their lips met, the world outside the closed restaurant seemed to fade away, leaving only the soft glow of the dimmed interior lights.

The kiss lingered for a moment, a sweet culmination of unspoken emotions building between them. When they finally pulled away, Garwin smiled and looked into Erin's eyes.

"I guess that's one way to end the night," he said, a hint of playfulness in his voice.

Erin returned the smile, feeling a warmth spreading through her. "It was unexpected, but I can't say I'm complaining."

"You know, the sooner we set a date, the sooner we can get our wedding night going," Garwin said.

Erin nodded, "You know that when the wedding night is over, you'll be stuck with me."

Garwin nodded, "I know. The thought doesn't scare me. Does it scare you?"

"No." Erin shook her head, "not at all."

Chapter Nineteen

It was quite by accident that Erin discovered Miss Enid had an impressive orchard at the back of the house and a hammock strategically placed between two mango trees.

So, after collecting more oranges and lemons than she had ever seen outside of a commercial setting, she went into the hammock, running through all the recipes she could make with oranges; lemons were easy, and there were lots of applications for lemons.

And then her mind wandered as it always did to her imaginary wedding and honeymoon. She spent most of her free time doing this, imagining being married to Garwin and sleeping with him. She closed her eyes and imagined him peeling off her clothes piece by piece and then caressing her…

"Erin?" Rafi's voice sounded in her ear. Erin jumped. The hammock started rocking to and fro.

"What are you doing here?" she asked, clutching the sides of the hammock until it settled down.

"Your side gate was open," Rafi smiled.

"I thought you were in St. Lucia," Erin said.

"I was," Rafi said, "sorted out my business. I also found Heather and the ring."

"That's great," Erin said.

"Not so great," Rafi frowned. "My father found her first. That man is always a step ahead of me. And here I was, thinking I was working stealthily. I think Hal is working with him."

She's alive?"

"Yes," Rafi said, "still alive. Apparently, my father's goons roughed her up some, but he now has the ring. When I saw her, she was tearful and fearful. She told me to tell you she was sorry."

"Oh," Erin said. "Apology accepted, I guess. I found the phone. My cousin's son has been collecting shiny gold stuff and stashing them away. Let me go and get it. You can delete the video and check that I have never shared it. So, no blaming me if that video gets out."

"Okay," Rafi said.

"I am serious," Erin said, "tell your dad that Erin McMillan never shared that video."

Rafi chuckled. "I'll tell him."

He followed her into the house and sat in the drawing room while she searched her purse.

"I heard this place is for sale. Maybe I should buy it."

"Why would you want to live up here?" Erin asked.

"It's a really nice community," Rafi said. "I can see the appeal."

"It's okay. It's not that amazing," Erin said.

Rafi laughed. "I know you don't want me up here, Erin. I was joking."

"Good," Erin said. She handed him the phone. "There is

the video."

Rafi watched it to the end. "And you haven't shown anybody?"

"Not a soul," Erin said. "You do realize that Heather has a copy of it, don't you?"

"No, she doesn't," Rafi said. "She had it on her work phone, and all her personal phones were wiped. As I said, my father found her first. His people tortured her a little and frightened her a lot. I doubt she would want to mess with us again."

Erin shuddered.

"Are you sure you won't take me up on my offer to marry you, Erin?"

"Quite sure," Erin said.

Rafi nodded. "Well, have a great life. You deserve it."

"You too." Erin watched him as he walked down the driveway.

Not even a hint of remorse was in her thoughts as she saw the back of him. If she never saw him again, she would be quite fine.

She wondered if she should tell Garwin there was no need to get married again. She owed it to him to tell him the truth. She didn't want him to marry her under the false assumption that he would be helping her out.

It wasn't a conversation she was looking forward to. Her fantasies of being Mrs. Garwin Silver were dead.

She was pretty sure that Garwin would not want to marry her now without the sense of obligation to protect her.

****

Garwin scored the lone goal for the evening. The charity match was well attended. After the millionth congratulations and slap on his back, he opened his car door, chucking in his gear. He would go home, shower, and then visit Erin.

He hadn't seen her all day. He was about to open the driver's door when he felt a tap on his shoulder.

"Garwin, is it?" It was Rafi Chan, without a doubt. They really had a strong family resemblance.

It was the first time they were seeing each other face to face.

"I thought you were in St. Lucia," Garwin said.

"I wrapped up my business early, came to give Erin the good news."

"You found the ring?" Garwin murmured.

"I did." Rafi nodded. "And before I left Crimson Hills, never to darken its doors again, I decided to see the guy who I looked so much alike."

"I look like my mom," Garwin said.

"I know," Rafi said. "She looked like her father. It's nice to meet you, Garwin."

"I can't say the same, Rafi." Garwin frowned. "You threatened Erin. You were forcing her to marry you."

"That was before I got back the ring," Rafi said. "Now my business with Erin is done. You know, there is no need for us to be estranged. Now that you know who your mother is. Your grandmother feels like my grandmother, too. I treat her as such. She would love nothing better than to have the family coming together."

"I don't think I'd be comfortable," Garwin said, "at least not while your father is alive. You guys operate on a darker frequency than I am used to. My siblings and I are quite fine being the outsiders. At least now we know the Chans exist, and we should avoid getting involved with any of them romantically."

Rafi nodded. "I understand. See you around, Garwin."

They shook hands.

Garwin drove home. The thought assailed him; now that the reason to get married was pulled out from beneath their feet, did he still want to?

Would Erin still want to marry him? Now that she was free?

He would wait for her to say something just to test the waters. He wouldn't go to her house tonight or discuss the topic until she did.

Chapter Twenty

"**G**arwin has been avoiding me," Erin said to Patti. It was closing time, and Patti was waiting for Gresham in the restaurant's seating area while Erin was leaving. She was engrossed in her laptop, so Erin wondered if she even heard her.

Patti looked up at Erin and frowned. "How is that possible? You two work together, and you are getting married."

"He is taking breakfast and lunch times. I come in for the dinner service. He arranged the roster to avoid me. This has been going on for five days. We haven't even talked; we only text. He hasn't taken any of my calls."

"That's odd," Patti frowned. "Previously, he couldn't get enough of you, Erin. It's always Erin this and Erin that."

"Oh, so he hasn't told you?" Erin sat down across from Patti. "Rafi came by; he found his precious ring, and I found my phone, and he deleted the video. All is well in Rafi Chan's world."

"Oh," Patti nodded. "So there is no need for marriage,

then?"

"None," Erin said.

"So why aren't you happy?" Patti asked. "You are free to go anywhere you want to; you don't have to hide anymore, and Garwin doesn't have to marry you to protect you."

"Well," Patti frowned, "I wouldn't mind going through with it. I love Garwin; I want to marry him!"

"Okay," Patti leaned back in her seat. "So why don't you tell him, then? The mature thing to do would be to go to his house, knock on his door, and tell him."

"No," Erin shook her head. "That's too... too... brazen. What if he is relieved that he doesn't have to go through with it? I don't want to guilt him into marriage. It's not as if we told anyone what we were about to do anyway. It's not like we sent out wedding invitations or anything like that."

"That was smart," Patti nodded. "Maybe you can both ignore things and return to how you were."

"Yep," Erin nodded.

"Or you can talk it out, tell him that you love him and want to work things out."

"Or," Erin mused, "I can visit my parents in Cayman, chill for a while, find another job somewhere else."

"Oh no," Patti shook her head. "That won't do. You have to stay here and face things together. Why are you young people so fickle?"

"Didn't you leave Gersham here in Crimson Hills?" Erin asked.

"Yes," Patti nodded.

"And aren't we the same age?" Erin asked.

"The same physical age," Patti said, "mentally, I am an old woman. So you have to listen to me; I am wiser."

"Okay," Erin chuckled. "I am listening."

"I believe Garwin is feeling the same way you are," Patti

said. "He doesn't know how you feel; he is probably waiting for you to make a move. He is the one who came up with the idea of marriage. He said he had to convince you. Maybe he is wondering what you think now, and he doesn't want to rush you into something you didn't want in the first place."

"Okay, I'll go over to his place and talk things through," Erin said. "Wish me luck."

"I don't think you'll need it," Patti said.

****

It was her first time visiting the Silver residence, which was weird; especially since she had a relationship with Garwin. She had never been to his home. She knew which side was his; his vehicle was parked there. She leaned her bicycle at the front of his house, stepped onto the veranda, and knocked on the door. She was assailed with doubts: What if he didn't want to see her? What if he was in there with a girl?

She took a step back and then another. Maybe this wasn't a good idea.

"Erin!" Garwin dragged the door open; he was shirtless in lounge pants, his hair tousled.

"Hey."

"Hey," Erin said awkwardly. "You have been avoiding me."

"Come on in," Garwin opened the door wider.

She walked through. It was a nice place, modernly decorated in off-white with a splash of color here and there. The living room had a cozy atmosphere, with a black couch and a coffee table adorned with a few well-placed books. Erin noticed a faint aroma of pineapple and mango, something tropical, lingering in the air, like a scented candle.

She didn't know Garwin was into scented candles.

Garwin gestured towards the couch. "Have a seat. Can I get you something to drink?"

"Uh, sure, water is fine," Erin replied, feeling a mix of nervousness and relief as she took a seat.

Garwin disappeared into the kitchen, which was separated from the living room by an arch. Erin glanced around the room. Evidently, he had put effort into making it a comfortable space. It was decorated in black and white, with cute pictures on the wall. She fidgeted with her fingers, still grappling with the uncertainty of why she was there.

Garwin returned with a shirt on and a glass of water and sat across from her, his expression a curious mix of concern and confusion. "So, what brings you here?"

Erin took a deep breath, trying to steady her nerves. "I just... I felt like we needed to talk. Things have been weird between us lately since Rafi found his ring..."

Garwin nodded. "Yeah, I needed some time to think. I didn't mean to avoid you, Erin."

Erin cleared her throat. "Should we talk about the 'married' elephant in the room?"

A brief silence hung in the air, and then Garwin spoke, breaking the tension. "I'm sorry, I was trying to answer the question: Is this love that I'm feeling."

"The Bob Marley song." Erin nodded, "You could have told me, Garwin, that you are grappling with this latest development. We're supposed to be friends, right?"

He sighed, running a hand through his tousled hair. "You're right, and I should have. I didn't mean to shut you out. Friends don't do that to each other, but I answered the question and was psyching myself up to approach you with the answer."

Erin inhaled loudly. "Wait, don't tell me. If you give me a

'Dear Erin' speech, I might lose it. I would prefer that over text."

Garwin laughed. "Why?"

"Because I love you, and the truth is, I was looking forward to marrying you; it was real for me, and…"

Garwin put a finger over her lips. "I love you and want to still marry you if you'll have me. I have run through several arguments in my head these past couple of days and the one that is more pressing is that I don't want to live without you."

Erin smiled. "The feeling is mutual."

"You have no idea how I missed seeing you every day," Garwin murmured. "I wanted to see how long I could go before I broke down and…"

Erin reached across and kissed him. "Don't do this again."

"I won't," Garwin whispered. "Erin will you marry me?"

"Of course," she smiled.

Epilogue

Eight weeks later

The grand opening of the Silver Spoon entertainment venue was marked with a chef's wedding. It was packed with Garwin and Erin's family and friends. It was only fitting that the chefs were the first to host an event there with their wedding and reception.

The space was transformed into a magical setting for Garwin and Erin's wedding ceremony, adorned with elegant decorations and surrounded by the warmth of their loved ones. All eyes turned towards the entrance where Erin, adorned in a breathtaking gown, appeared on her father's arm.

The new pergola, decorated with tons of sweet-smelling flowers, was where they exchanged vows.

The ceremony seamlessly transitioned into a lively reception. The atmosphere was one of pure joy.

Garwin and Erin shared their first dance as a married

couple, moving gracefully to the rhythm of Rob Orbison's "You Got It," a song that held a special place in their hearts.

"You okay?" Garwin whispered in her ear as they swung to the music.

"I couldn't be better," Erin smiled. "Best day of my life so far."

"Mine too," Garwin said, holding her tight and whispering words only meant for her ears. "When we first met, I never imagined we'd end up here, dancing as husband and wife. I used to think I had no time for love, but I found the time with you."

Erin gazed into Garwin's eyes, feeling the warmth of their shared history and the promise of a future together.

Garwin continued, "I can't wait to see what adventures await us, Erin. With you, every day is an incredible journey."

Erin rested her head on Garwin's shoulder, savoring the moment and the sweet connection they shared. The dance floor seemed like their private world, where time stood still. The melody wrapped around them, creating a cocoon of happiness.

As the song's final notes echoed through the venue, Garwin looked deep into her eyes. "Here's to many more dances, my love, and countless more memories together," he said, sealing the sentiment with a tender kiss.

The End

Why did he let his therapist convince him to come to Crimson Hills? Chex thought darkly as he sat in the back of the town car on the way to his father's funeral. He didn't need closure; he wasn't grieving. He felt nothing, really. He had escaped the place when he was sixteen and had legally changed his name from Knight to Hastings when he was eighteen. Since he had left twenty years ago, he had not been back to Knightsbridge, their seventy-acre farm in the hills.

"Why did you leave up here in the first place?" Dana asked chirpily. "It's gorgeous! I could see myself doing a vacation here. Do you know what this place reminds me of? Taormina in Sicily. It's the rolling hills and the sea in the distance."

Chex sighed; Dana had insisted on coming with him instead of traveling on the coaster that the Hastings family had hired to transport the clan to support his mother. Dana was one of the Hastings cousins. His grandfather, Eustace, had one child, Lauralee, Chex's mom, but Eustace's siblings had dozens of children, and Dana was one of them. Her home base was in New York, but she was always traveling. He had casually mentioned to her that Maurice had died and Dana had booked a flight to the funeral. She was staying in the guest house at the Hastings mansion. He had taken her partying the night before, mostly so that he didn't have to talk about his father's passing. She was the type who thought people should talk about their feelings twenty four seven.

He didn't know why people thought he would be feeling some sort of remorse when Maurice died. He would have preferred not to even acknowledge it. His father had been dead and buried in his head for years now. He was itching to tell Danger to turn the car around and head back to Kingston. Attending this funeral would be a farce. His mother had Phillip and Jack to lean on for support. She didn't need him. He would be of no use. The love of her life had been the bane of his existence. He would rather dance on his father's grave than weep.

What on earth was he doing? He wasn't going through with this.

"I am not doing this," he said out loud.

Dana looked at him, confused. "But we are almost there. That sign says Three Miles to Knightsbridge Farm."

Chex inhaled.

"Boss? Danger slowed down and looked at him curiously.

"We'll drop Dana, then we are going back."

"So, who will I go back to Kingston with?" Dana pouted.

"Phillip and Pearl," Chex said through gritted teeth. He was feeling a little lightheaded the closer they got to the farm. "Or you can take the bus with the rest of the family."

Dana frowned. "Why do you sound so breathless?"

"Stop the car," Chex said weakly.

Danger stopped the car.

Chex closed his eyes. He felt strange like he wasn't getting enough oxygen. Was this a panic attack?

"There is a restaurant up ahead," Danger's voice sounded like it was coming from a distance. "It says Silver Spoon Restaurant. Want me to leave you there and then come back?"

"Yes," Chex nodded. He kept his eyes closed, willing the feeling to pass.

"It's pretty over here," Dana whistled. "Maybe I should stay with you. Who wants to go to a stuffy old funeral anyway?”

"Go," Chex cracked an eye open. "You came all this way."

"And so did you," Dana said.

"Coming was a mistake," Chex said hoarsely. "I shouldn't have come; this was a bad call by my therapist. It's like returning to the crime scene where you were the victim."

Dana nodded. "So the rumors were true?"

"What rumors?" Chex asked.

"That Maurice tied you up on a cross and whipped you until you couldn't move?" Dana inhaled, "Or that he had a house on the property called punishment house where he locked you in the dark and starved you until you told him what he wanted to hear?"

"Sounds about right," Chex got out of the car. "That's why I ran away from home at sixteen, and when the police brought me back, I refused to leave the car. They had to take me to the station until Grandpa Eustace came for me."

"Why didn't Lauralee do something?" Dana whispered, her eyes bright with unshed tears.

"Whenever she did," Chex said, "he would up my punishment. He didn't want her to love us more than him. He was rabidly jealous of her attention."

"Why didn't she leave?" Dana whispered.

"Because she loved him back," Chex inhaled. "Nothing could shake that love. I have never understood it. Maybe you can ask her when you see her. I don't think I can face her right now or this farce of a funeral."

He slammed the door and headed toward the restaurant. He couldn't recall any of the businesses on the lower part of the hills, except Wimples Bakery, but it made sense that there would be development to cater to the tourists and the locals who lived up in the hills. Maybe when Danger came back, he would take a drive around.

He entered the restaurant with its warm and inviting atmosphere. It looked like any high-end place in Kingston. The smell of fried chicken greeted him as soon as he stepped inside. He hadn't tasted good home-cooked fried chicken in ages. He wasn't even hungry; he had just wanted a break. Now, after smelling the chicken, he definitely would order something. Soft reggae music played in the background, adding to the atmosphere of the place.

A hostess greeted him with a warm smile as he approached. "Table for one?" she asked politely.

Chex nodded, "Yes, please."

He followed her through the bustling restaurant, the chatter of other patrons providing a temporary reprieve from the heaviness on his mind. He settled into a corner booth; he could see the door from where he was and the gardens where he sat.

His mind kept going back to the question Dana had posed about Lauralee. "Why didn't your mother do something?"

He had asked her the same question over the years but never got a satisfactory answer. Why couldn't she have loved them enough to leave Maurice? He had never had a mother's love. Maybe that was why he treated women shabbily.

He'd see what his therapist thought about that theory; Dr. Henry would probably tell him that he was on the right track, connecting the dots between his tumultuous past and the way it shaped his present.

The hostess gave him a menu with a reassuring smile, interrupting his thoughts momentarily.

"Your server will be right with you. Enjoy your meal," she said, leaving Chex to peruse the menu again.

Chex studied the menu, his mind swirled with childhood memories he would rather not dwell on.

"Neon!" He heard a familiar voice screech at the door.

"Halt! Run, don't walk!"

He looked up from the menu, and his heart stopped beating. It screeched to a halt. He was feeling lightheaded and dizzy again.

There was Garnet at the door of the restaurant. Garnet Silver. The one that had gotten away. The one woman who had made him contemplate giving up the constant partying. The only person he had ever confided in with all of his feelings. He had 'done' feelings with her. He had thought what they had was real.

There she was, standing at the door. She had walked out on him and never looked back, and he had forced himself not to follow her or beg her to come back.

Her hair was longer than he had ever seen; she was dressed in jean shorts and a tank top, and she wore large shades, typical Garnet attire. She looked prettier than ever if that was possible.

"Mommy, please, can I have ice cream?" The curly-haired little boy was talking to her. "Mommy, please."

What on earth was going on? Chex straightened up in his seat, shock ricocheting through him. Garnet had a kid?

And why was it that the kid looked like a dead ringer for Maurice Knight?

Phillip looked like Maurice. Had Garnet had an affair with his older brother?

And then the boy turned in his direction, his eyes were the color of light amber.

His grandfather used to theorize that Chex got the eyes from his father, Alex Hastings and was therefore unique. Nobody else in the family had his eyes. Not one out of the myriad of cousins or his brothers.

And this kid had his eyes!

Maurice and Phillip's face, his eyes, Garnet had some

explaining to do…

Discover Exclusive Offers and Be the First to Know!

If you haven't already, don't miss out on the opportunity to join my New Release Newsletter! Sign up today and become part of an exclusive community where you'll be among the first to hear about my latest book releases and take advantage of special prices.

Why join my mailing list?

Be the First: Get a head start and be the first to know when I release a new book.

Exclusive Discounts: Unlock special prices available only to subscribers. Enjoy limited time offers and save big on your favorite books.

Quick and Easy: Signing up takes less than 30 seconds.

To join, visit https://www.brenalbar.com/newsletter or scan the QR code below.

Thank you for your support, and happy reading!

The Crimson Hill Series

Where family drama, romance, and a touch of sci-fi blend seamlessly in the enchanting backdrop of a small town in Jamaica. Prepare to embark on an unforgettable journey as secrets unravel, passions ignite, and destinies intertwine.

No Goodbye (Book 1)
No Misunderstanding (Book 2)
No Ordinary Love (Book 3)
No Fairy Tale (Book 4)
No Letting Go (Book 5)
No Strings Attached (Book 6)
No More Mrs. Nice Girl (Book 7)
No Place Like You (Book 8)
Knight and Day (Book 8.5)
No Expectations (Book 9)
Ice and Fyre (Book 9.5)
No Surrender (Book 10)
No Time for Love (Book 11)
No Promises (Book 12)
Winter's Eve (Book 13)

The Wiley Brothers

Step into the world of the Wiley Brothers, where tragedy weaves an unbreakable bond and love becomes their guiding light. In this captivating series, follow the journey of six remarkable boys as they navigate the tumultuous path   of growing up without parents, discovering love, and finding their place in a challenging world.

Between Brothers (Book 0)- How it all began…
For Pete's Sake (Book 1)- Preston's story.
Crossing Jordan (Book 2)-Jordan's story.
Fire and Walter (Book 3)- Walter's story.
The Perfect Guy (Book 4)-Guy's Story.
The Patience of a Saint (Book 5)- Saint's Story.
A Case of Love (Book 6)- Case's Story.

The Pryce Sisters

Follow the remarkable journey of the Pryce triplets as they navigate the complexities of growing up, discovering romance, and embracing the exhilarating challenges of the new adult years.

Baby For A Pryce- Book 1
Right Pryce Wrong Time – Book 2
Yours, For A Pryce- Book 3

The Jacksons

Prepare to be enthralled by the captivating saga of the Jackson family. In this gripping series, secrets unravel, paternity questions loom, and love blooms in the most unexpected corners.

Ace- Book 1
Deuce- Book 2
Trey- Book 3
Quade- Book 4

The Scarlett Series

Their patriarch died and unexpectedly left each of them a fortune. Watch as the Scarlett family navigate their way through the ups and downs of sudden wealth, family secrets, and the complicated dynamics of their relationships.

Scarlett Baby (Book 1)
Scarlett Sinner (Book 2)
Scarlett Secret (Book 3)
Scarlett Love (Book 4)
Scarlett Promise (Book 5)
Scarlett Bride (Book 6)
Scarlett Heart (Book 7)

Magnolia Sisters

They were the rejects. The worst of the lot, they grew up in a girl's home together and formed sisterly bonds. Each book in the series tells the story of a different girl and the unique struggles and triumphs she faces along the way. With themes of friendship, forgiveness, and the power of love, the "Magnolia Sisters" series is a heartwarming and inspiring read that you won't want to put down.

Dear Mystery Guy- Book 1
Bad Girl Blues- Book 2
Her Mistaken Dream- Book 3
Just Like Yesterday – Book 4

New Song Series

A group of friends started out as a church band, see how each of them navigate their personal and professional lives while staying true to their faith and facing challenges along the way. With themes of forgiveness, redemption, and second chances, the New Song Series is a captivating read for anyone who enjoys heartwarming stories of love and faith.

Going Solo- Book 1
Duet on Fire- Book 2
Tangled Chords- Book 3
Broken Harmony- Book 4
A Past Refrain- Book 5
Perfect Melody- Book 6

The Bancrofts

The Bancroft family delves into the inner workings of academia and the high-stakes world of university politics. The family wrestles with the pressures of maintaining their family's legacy, they must confront their own demons and navigate the complex relationships that bind them together. From unexpected love affairs and betrayals to scandals and secrets that threaten to tear them apart, this is a series that will keep you captivated until the very end.

Homely Girl- Book 0
Saving Face- Book 1
Tattered Tiara- Book 2
Private Dancer- Book 3
Goodbye Lonely- Book 4
Practice Run- Book 5
Sense of Rumor- Book 6
A Younger Man- Book 7
Just To See Her- Book 8

Three Rivers Series

Three Rivers Series, a captivating tale of love, redemption, and second chances set in a picturesque community in St. Ann's Bay, Jamaica.

Private Sins- Book 1
Loving Mr. Wright- Book 2
Unholy Matrimony- Book 3
If It Ain't Broke- Book 4

The Resetter Series

The Resetter Series takes a look at a rare kind of person, a person who can travel back in time, but they only have one chance to get things right if they go back! With themes of second chances, changing the past and the power of love, the resetters series is a captivating time travel romance that many readers have described as a page turner.

Never Too Late- Book 1
Never Say Never- Book 2
Now or Never- Book 3
Almost Never- Book 4

On the Rebound Series

Experience the gripping and emotionally charged On the Rebound series, where love, betrayal, and redemption collide in a whirlwind of passion and secrets.
Brace yourself for a journey filled with drama, cheating scandals, DNA questions, and ultimately, the power of second chances and finding love again.

On the Rebound- Book 1
On the Rebound Book 2

Standalone Books

Full Circle- After graduating from university, Diana wanted to return to Jamaica to find her siblings. What she didn't foresee was that she would meet Robert Cassidy and that both their pasts would be intertwined, and that disturbing questions would pop up about their parentage just when they were getting close.

After the End- Torn between two lovers. Colleen married her high school sweetheart, Isaiah, hoping that they would live happily ever after, but life intruded, and Isaiah disappeared at sea. She found work with the rich and handsome Enrique Lopez as a housekeeper and realized that she couldn't keep him at arm's length.

Love Triangle: Three Sides to the Story- George, the husband. Marie, the wife, and Karen-the mistress. They all get to tell their side of the story.

New Beginnings- Inner-city girl Geneva was offered an opportunity of a lifetime when she learned that her 'real' father was a wealthy man. Her decision to live up-town meant she had to leave Froggie, her 'ghetto don,' behind. She also found herself battling with her stepmother and battling her emotions for Justin, a suave up-towner.

The Preacher and the Prostitute- Prostitution and the clergy don't mix. Tell that to ex-prostitute Maribel, who finds herself in love with the Pastor at her church. Can an ex-prostitute and a pastor have a future together?

Historical Fiction

You won't want to miss out on these two captivating reads!

"The Pull of Freedom" tells the story of a slave family and their desperate struggle for freedom in Jamaica's colonial era. Follow the journey of these brave individuals as they fight for their right to be free, facing danger, heartbreak, and unimaginable obstacles along the way.

"The Empty Hammock" takes readers on a journey through time, as a modern woman finds herself transported back to the Taino era of Jamaica's history. Experience the wonder and mystery of this ancient culture through her eyes, as she learns about their traditions, beliefs, and way of life. With richly drawn characters and a beautifully realized setting, "The Empty Hammock" is a must-read for anyone who loves historical fiction that transports them to another time and place.

Short Story Collections

Di Taxi Ride and Other Stories- Funny stories about Jamaican life to make you laugh.